Chasing Ivan

AN ACHILLES NOVELLA

Tim Tigner

For Elena. Here we go again, my love…

Chapter 1

Hanging Out

I LOVE CLIMBING. Give me a cliff face and a bag of climbing chalk and I'll be whistling all the way to the top.

But I had no chalk today.

No cliff face either.

I was 200 feet up one of London's famous residential towers, clinging to the weathered stone in a dove gray business suit.

For the last eight weeks, I'd been tailing a couple of people while waiting for a legend to strike. That legend was a Russian criminal mastermind known as Ivan the Ghost, a man so skilled in the art of invisibility, his very existence was in doubt.

The CIA's new director had learned that Ivan was planning to rig the upcoming London mayoral election by forcing the leading candidate to withdraw. Director Rider was eager to exploit this rare intelligence coup to score political points and eliminate Ivan. Permanently and covertly. That was where I came in, as a member of the CIA's Special Operations Group.

Ivan didn't use guns or gangsters, and he never left a trail or trace. He concocted elaborate schemes — traps that caught his victims unaware and kept them silent. Creative coercions and invisible operations were his trademarks, his sources of pride and fame.

We expected Ivan to strike at the mayoral candidate through one of two relatives, either his daughter Emily, or his brother Evan. But that was just a guess. Still, we were thrilled that for once, for the first time, we just might be one step ahead of The Ghost.

"Have you got eyes on him yet?" Oscar asked.

Oscar Pincus, my control back at Langley, was sporadically monitoring the situation via my earpiece. Oscar had just joined the Agency. A pet placed in a plum role by a new director more concerned with influence than competence.

Oscar and I had both become excited when our electronic surveillance picked up Evan lying to his office manager about an appointment we knew he didn't have. Our hearts really started racing when he slipped away to an apartment on the nineteenth floor of the luxury residence to which I now clung. Our hope and expectation was that his clandestine meeting was part of a cleverly construed trap arranged by Ivan. "I made it up to nineteen. Now I just have to climb over to unit B."

"So that's a *no*. Ivan's finally about to strike, and

we're blind."

I didn't reply. I didn't have time for Oscar right now. My current position was more than physically precarious. The British government didn't know I was here. In fact, I'd be screwed if they found out. Indoctrination into the SOG came with the warning that the US government will disavow agents to avoid embarrassment.

Disavow.

What a term.

It's the grown-up equivalent to shrugging. But then that's politics, which resembles espionage, in that it revolves around lies. The difference, incidentally, is that spies don't smile while lying.

I got a grip on the rail of the nineteenth-floor balcony, and began sliding left, hand to hand. I kept my legs raised out to the side as I went. That way, the residents of the eighteenth floor wouldn't see them dangling while enjoying the view over afternoon tea.

It was a clear day, so from that altitude I could see the city skyscrapers to the south, and the sun reflecting off The Regent's Park boating lake to the west. Theoretically, that meant millions of people could see me as well. Good thing I was wearing gray.

With forty meters to cover and not a second to spare, my hands slipped into a familiar climbing rhythm. Quick but cautious. As a free-solo enthusiast, I was used to climbing without ropes or tools. The business suit, however, was working against me. It bottled in heat, which brought on the enemy. It wasn't only job interviews where sweaty palms could be deadly.

The fresh pigeon poop wasn't helping either.

I'd just rounded the corner when crescendoing screams from the balcony below shattered the still air. "Oh my God! Oh my God! Oh my God! William! William!" Looking down as my heart regained its normal rhythm, I saw that the afternoon sun had cast my shadow in the wrong place at the wrong time. A silver-haired woman stared back at me, her mouth agape and her eyes bugged wide, watering the floor rather than her geraniums.

I always tried to smile in the face of adversity. In this case the smile was literal. "It's okay, luv," I said, invoking a gentlemanly British accent. "I slipped, but caught myself."

I pulled myself up onto the balcony above her with a couple of quick, fluid moves, and then peered back over to reassure her. "No worries. I'm quite safe now, luv."

As I ducked back, I heard her speaking to somebody. Then an elderly male voice said, "I'm calling the police."

Bloody hell. The response time to an intruder alert at a posh place like this would be minutes.

I dropped to the balcony floor and began a rapid low-crawl toward unit 19-B. Looking over my right shoulder through the glass wall of the flat I'd just invaded, I spotted a pigtailed girl playing with colorful figurines.

She was seated facing the kitchen, where her mother was busy chopping vegetables. If her mom looked up, the police would get another frantic call and I'd likely end up playing aerial hide-and-seek with a helicopter.

I made it to the wall that separated my current location from Evan's without drawing her eye. While that was good news, the barrier before me was not. The architect had made it virtually impossible for even the bold and the brave to use the balconies to hop between flats.

I was going to have to go back over the rail and shimmy along the edge again. But I'd have to do it between floors nineteen and twenty this time since the couple on eighteen was likely watching their window, anxiously anticipating more excitement.

Still praying that the girl's mother wouldn't look up from her knife, I climbed onto the balcony rail, braced myself with my left hand against the wall, and mapped out my jump. To reach the lip of the balcony above, I was going to have to spring up about two feet and back about one.

The vertical jeopardy that jump presented would paralyze most people, but competitive climbers are a different breed. We're born with the ability to disconnect the acrophobia circuit and operate in the air as if on the ground. Put another way, a jump from a ledge is just a jump, if one doesn't think about the drop.

I gave my palms a good wipe on my thighs. Then I crouched down, breathed deep, and rocketed up, my arms swinging into it and adding momentum as my legs exploded and my eyes locked on target.

Oscar's voice sounded in my ear. "Whom were you talking to?"

The jolt knocked me off balance, just a bit, but enough that correcting it cost me power. My grasp came up a quarter-inch short of the ornamental lip, with my fingertips barely grazing its edge.

Now I was thinking about that drop.

As my upward momentum began the rapid transition to a downward plummet, I seesawed my shoulders, thrusting my right arm up while dipping my left. This practiced move added precisely two-and-a-quarter inches to my extension, enough to get the last digit of two fingers over the lip in time. The moment they touched, I cleared my mind of all other thought. I became those two fingertips, rooting in and holding fast. I remained in that meditative state until the rest of my body stabilized like a coat hanging from a hook. Then, with a slow and steady exhale, I brought my thumb up to crimp the hold, and pulled my left arm up beside its twin.

"Hold on, Oscar," I said, hoping he'd appreciate the need for my focus to be elsewhere.

That wasn't a given.

Oscar had about as much experience in the field as I had managing public relations. Zero.

After a couple of deep breaths, I resumed the hand-to-hand swinging shuffle toward 19-B, still focusing on my fingers but with my ears also primed for the sound of sirens. A few seconds later, I swung my legs forward and dropped onto the proper balcony, relieved and ready for more conventional action.

A fortuitous gap in the bedroom's beige curtains beckoned, and I advanced with caution. I peered through at waist-level and saw them immediately. Evan and his secret date were naked on the bed.

Bad news.

Even in her state of undress, I had no problem identifying the petite redhead. Sarah Simms was a weather girl at one of the local TV stations.

Crap.

This wasn't Ivan's trap. There was no leverage here. Evan was divorced, and Sarah had just appeared on one of the social rags' *Most Eligible* lists.

"False alarm," I said to Oscar.

"Not a teenage boy?" Oscar asked.

"Or a Mafia wife."

"Drugs?"

"I can't be certain without breaching, but I think we can assume that Evan is purely testosterone driven. She's hot. A local weather girl."

"I dated a weather girl once," Oscar said.

As he continued with a sexual pun, my phone vibrated an alert. I heard a simultaneous beep on Oscar's end. "What is it?" I asked him.

"Tonight's the night of Emily's big date, right? Her first encounter with the mysterious Andreas she won't stop talking about?"

"That's right."

"Well, her phone just went dead."

Chapter 2

Foreplay

EMILY YELPED as her cell phone flew from her grasp and sailed out over the boating lake. Rubbing the back of her hand while the oblivious bike messenger zipped on to some northwest London business address, she watched her phone land flat on the still water.

For a joyful second, it looked as if it was going to float, but as Emily plunged in after it like a Labrador chasing a stick, her phone went under. By the time she'd snatched it from the lake the display had gone blank. Probably not a good sign, she figured.

Still standing thigh-deep in murky water, she pulled off the protective cover and began shaking it like a maraca, trying to expel water from the speakers and ports, while passersby looked on sympathetically.

"Don't turn it on!" a red-haired boy of middle-school years yelled from the path. "Give it a couple of days to dry out first. Maybe you'll get lucky."

"Bake it on low in the oven," his freckled friend

added. "That will help."

She gave them a kind nod. "Thanks."

Would Jen think she'd hung up on her? Emily wondered. *Possibly.*

They'd been at it again over Andreas.

Her best friend had been cautioning her for the hundredth time not to get her hopes up, while Emily reasserted her certainty that he wouldn't turn out to be a gold digger like the others.

Emily had argued that Andreas didn't know her last name. Therefore, he didn't know who her father was, and thus he wouldn't have any ulterior motives. Plus, he just felt different. He felt perfect — as if he'd been designed with her tastes and interests in mind. In any case, she'd find out for sure in just a few hours. After two months of online dating, of long emails, and shared secrets, and rising expectations, they were finally going to meet.

She'd been thinking about little else for weeks.

Emily was determined not to let either Jen's cautionary words or a ruined phone spoil her mood. Life only gave you so many magical moments. No sense ruining them with mundane worries.

She slipped the phone and cover into her purse, and continued her walk north across the park toward her favorite grocer. Her soggy sandals slapped the pavement with each step, while the water soaking her yoga pants slowly worked its way up toward her crotch. She'd wash both as soon as she got home to get the lake smell out.

Her block of flats, Palace Place, wasn't nearly as regal as its name, but it did have a nice lobby. Comfortable chairs in a window alcove. Decent original oils on the walls. Various English seascapes painted by widow Cooper in 3B. The white cliffs of Dover. The beach at West Wittering. Sunset over the Isle of Wight. Mrs. Cooper had been updating them over time as her skill increased, and now the familiar sight of them was as welcoming as a wink and a smile.

Emily winced as the shopping bag shifted while she reached for the handle on the lobby door. The back of her hand was tender where the messenger's backpack had whacked it. She hoped it wouldn't bruise and look ugly for Andreas.

"Let me help you with that," came a voice from behind as a long arm reached past and opened the front door. "After you."

For a second Emily thought the gentleman might be Andreas, his earliness expressing the eagerness she felt. Dressed in a summer-weight gray suit, he was tall and athletic and about thirty. Check, check, and check. The thick, dark hair wasn't styled the same as in her suitor's profile picture, but hairstyles changed. This man's eyes were the same sparkling blue that had captured her attention. He also had the high Slavic cheekbones. The match was six for six when a distinct chin dimple ruled the gentleman out. She felt a stab of disappointment, but said, "Thank you."

Emily checked her postbox while he brushed past with a bow of his head before disappearing up the stairs. She was sure he wasn't a resident. Probably Justine's latest.

Emily hoped Justine would see Andreas when he arrived. Let her be the jealous one for once.

The knock came as Emily was putting the last of her purchases in the refrigerator. Again her mind leapt to an early arrival. She reached for her cell to check the time only to be greeted by a black screen. The clock on the microwave showed 1:48. Andreas wasn't due to pick her up for another four hours.

She slipped off her soggy sandals and crept to the peephole.

The man on the other side of the door doffed a chauffeur's cap with a white-gloved hand as she darkened the lens.

What in the world? Was her father up to something, or more likely, his slippery campaign manager?

She opened the door. "Yes?"

"Hello, Emily. I'm Michael. Andreas sent me."

She wasn't sure how to respond to that, and Michael continued before she decided.

"I'm afraid he won't be able to make it this evening."

Chapter 3

Carpe Diem

EMILY FELT her eyes start to tear as her heart sank.

Not again.

Not Andreas too.

Every time she got her hopes up, they were dashed. Every time.

Andreas had seemed so different, but Jen had been right. Well, at least it was a classy letdown. She didn't know he was wealthy — on top of everything else. More salt for her wound. "Thanks for letting me know."

The chauffeur didn't move.

Was she supposed to tip this guy?

"Andreas was hoping you could join him instead."

"What?"

"He's stuck out of town. He'd love you to join him. He's really been looking forward to meeting you. Honestly, I've never seen him so smitten."

Emily felt her chest reinflate as a smile lifted her cheeks to the sky. "Where is he?"

"About three hours from here. We'll need to leave right away. The limo is out front."

The limo is out front. How many times had that phrase passed through her fanciful mind as a schoolgirl imagining her Prince Charming? What was this guy's name? Had he said Michael? Feeling disoriented but brushing aside her own queries for now, she said, "I'm nowhere near ready. Look at me."

"You look lovely, and besides, you'll have plenty of time to get yourself together on the plane."

"The plane?"

"Just grab your passport. Andreas has arranged for everything else."

"What does that mean?" She spoke without thinking, and immediately feared that she'd sounded rude.

In response, Michael just smiled.

She began to wonder if the bicycle messenger had hit her head as well as her hand. Perhaps she was in a coma, dreaming all of this. If she was, she hoped she'd make it to the happy ending before waking. *If she wasn't, would she be crazy to consider this extraordinary proposition?*

She knew what Jen would say.

Jen would bring up all kinds of horror stories about murders and kidnappings. Emily didn't want to hear it, but figured she should at least let Jen know what was happening. She'd make it a quick call.

Reaching for her phone, she again remembered the

lake. She didn't have a phone, or even a number without access to her electronic address book.

As she was contemplating this twist to her unbelievable predicament, Michael raised his left hand, presenting a small pizza box made of black leather. He held it there for a second to let her suspense build, then he pulled back the lid to reveal a necklace that glowed like a spring morning. A magnificent golden sun pendant on a platinum rope. The ends of the rope fed through a large platinum moon clasp, and wrapped around a matching pair of earrings — a golden sun, and a platinum moon. "Andreas said you'd know the significance."

She did. It was her favorite line of poetry, a line he'd referenced in one of their early emails. Tears started streaming down her cheeks as she recited the line. "Tell me the story about how the Sun loved the Moon so much he died every night to let her breathe."

She reached out with both hands to lift the necklace from the box, fearing that she was about to pop the illusion. It was heavier than she'd expected, and by far the most beautiful piece of jewelry she'd ever touched. Clearly a different caliber from anything else in her modest box. She wasn't even certain how to work the fancy clasp.

"May I assist you?" Michael asked, holding out his free hand.

"Why don't you come in," Emily said, backing into

her woefully humble flat. Michael followed and she turned her back to him, lifting her chestnut ponytail while watching him in the wall mirror beside the door.

"The special clasp makes the length fully adjustable. I think that's about right. What do you think?"

Emily swapped out her simple gold earrings for the celestial bodies, and dropped her arms to admire the complete package. "I think it's perfect. I don't know what to say. I really need to change before we go. Although I'm not sure I have anything that will do them justice."

"That's all been taken care of."

Overwhelmed by the situation, she again spoke without thinking. "How is that possible? Andreas and I talked about a lot of things, but my dress size wasn't one of them."

"Your shoe size either, I expect, but then Andreas is a resourceful man. We really do need to be going."

Emily didn't want to get too analytical for fear she'd ruin everything. She had a choice to make. A simple *yes* or *no* decision, and yet as complicated as any she'd made.

She felt stuck and was frustrated with her own indecisiveness when the back of her mind kicked out a trick her mother had taught her way back when. *The right move became obvious when framed with the right question.* She asked herself what she would be feeling an hour from now, if she said *no*. "Give me two minutes to slip on some dry jeans."

Chapter 4

Suspect Motivations

I PUNCHED THE AIR with the elation of a big-game hunter spotting a fresh trail. "Bingo!"

I'd made it down the high-rise just before the police arrived, only to court disaster again by racing through three miles of central London traffic without regard for traffic signs. But the risks had paid off when I reached Palace Place in time to enter with Emily.

"Say again, Achilles." Oscar's voice was getting weak in my ear. The battery on my comm unit was dying.

"This could be it."

"Do you think Michael could be Ivan?" Oscar asked.

Oscar had heard the same promising discussion I had, despite being 4,000 miles away. "I didn't see him," I said. "But I seriously doubt it. The Ghost is too cautious not to use an intermediary at this stage."

"What do you mean you didn't see him? How could you miss him?"

"I was up in the third-floor hallway. After sticking the cricket on Emily's purse, I needed to disappear." Crickets were the CIA's latest listening devices — highly-sensitive, internally-powered bugs that also *chirped* a GPS signal, hence the name. The one I'd just placed would allow us to keep tabs on Emily until she got a new phone. Or changed her purse.

"And you chose to go into a blind spot, rather than back out to the street?"

"An about-face would have looked suspicious. I didn't know her date was going to show up four hours early. Don't worry though. I'll get film when they leave. I'm in the lobby now."

The mysterious Andreas had been our prime suspect from the beginning, but he'd taken so long to close the deal that we'd begun to think that he really was just an online suitor. Ironically, the most encouraging thing was that we hadn't been able to learn anything about him.

This last twist made me certain.

"You think she'll actually go? She might be desperate for dick, but how stupid do you have to be to fly overseas at the last minute for a blind date?"

Oscar was supposedly only a decade or so older than me, but sometimes I thought he was a defrosted Neanderthal. "She'll go because she's a romantic, and she's fallen for him."

"If he really was Casanova, or her motives really were pure, he wouldn't need the chauffeured limousine, private plane, and custom jewelry."

I'd been studying Ivan as a professional hobby for the better part of a year, which was how I'd landed the case when Director Rider got a lead. That and my Russian fluency. "He probably doesn't need those things. But probably isn't the same thing as definitely. The Ghost leaves nothing to chance. He never fails, and he's never detected, because he's extraordinarily meticulous.

"As for Emily, personally I'm convinced that she would happily ride on the back of a scooter to a chippy, so long as Andreas keeps the love-light burning."

Oscar chuffed loud enough for me to hear it. "Women. Where do you think they're going?"

"I don't know. But this changes things. Now we have to let Emily know what's going on."

"No way! Don't you even think about it, Achilles."

I've gone by my last name ever since I was a toddler.

For my third birthday, a family friend gave me a jersey with my name across the back, and I basically refused to take it off until my fourth. At which point the same friend gifted me a fresh one and my parents gave up all hope of ever calling me Kyle.

It also made for a good call sign.

"We don't know for certain that anything is going on," Oscar added, when I didn't reply immediately. "And if something is, then this is the first physical lead we've ever had on Ivan. You blow this for the sake of some British debutant, and Director Rider will show you the door faster than you can say *operational security*."

"She's not just leaving London. They're taking her out of the country. We don't know what kind of protection we'll be able to provide because we don't know where she's going."

"It doesn't matter. She's not in danger. Ivan's not violent. Killing clashes with his m.o."

"We don't know that he's not violent. We just surmise that from the crimes attributed to him."

"We're not telling her, Achilles. Drop it. At best, she'll freak out. At worst, she'll open her mouth and then Ivan really will kill her — right before he disappears. If you're worried about her, then you just plan on doing whatever it takes to keep her safe. Are we clear?"

God, how I missed Granger. I'd been stuck with Oscar for three missions now. I'd gone from working with one of the greatest legends in special operations, to working for a politician. I don't have anything against politicians, mind you. Well, that's not entirely true. At times, their disingenuous, self-serving nature makes me want to head-butt a window. But my issue with Oscar was that he didn't know what he didn't know.

Ignorance killed people in our line of work. The people in the field, that is. The armchair warriors back in Langley only had to weather the occasional paper cut. "Ivan will have his people deep-six her purse, you know. Just like he did her phone. No way that was a coincidence. They'll swap her old Coach bag for a fancy new one on the plane. Then we'll lose audio and GPS."

"So you'll just have to tag her again when you land. This time you can plan ahead for it, so you're not stuck hiding when all the action goes down."

I wanted to point out the stupidity of bumping into the same mark twice in the same day in two different cities, but didn't see any percentage in it. Oscar's only concern was the optics of the outcome. He didn't care how we got results, or even what results we got, so long as they made his boss look good.

CIA Director Wiley Rider was in desperate need of a few wins. His confirmation had been contentious and rocky. The president's first nominee to run the CIA had been both a darling of the Senate and a career veteran of the agency. Much to everyone's surprise, however, he'd withdrawn his name and then retired, citing personal reasons.

Rider, an outsider with substantial family wealth and great political ambitions, eventually secured confirmation only because the powerful head of the Senate Intelligence Committee pushed his name loudly and repeatedly and forcefully enough to eventually squeak him over the confirmation line.

In classic Washington style, the minute Rider was in the big office he began sweeping out the old guard to make room for his cronies. This included retiring

Granger in order to make room for Oscar.

Managing sensitive foreign threats to the American way of life now came second to making Rider shine. This op would do it. Nailing the globe's most clever and elusive criminal in his first hundred days would both put Rider's naysayers to shame, and give him enough political capital to coast on for years. He wouldn't care if a girl had to die to make that happen. She wasn't even American.

Chapter 5

Jet Set

EMILY COULDN'T STOP SMILING. Her trip down the rabbit hole into Andreas's wonderland was already the most exciting adventure of her life. And this was just the warm-up.

When Michael opened the limousine door to reveal the stairway to a private jet, she paused for one moment to steady her legs. Then another to soak it up.

Her elation turned to shame, Eliza Doolittle style, when she placed her sandaled foot with its two-week-old nail polish onto the red carpet that met the limo's door. She looked up at Michael, who returned a charitable expression.

"It has all been taken care of," he repeated, reading her mind.

If Andreas were even half the gentleman Michael was, Emily would think about kidnapping him.

A woman greeted her from atop the short, curved airstair. A twenty-something who looked as if she belonged. She had a fashion model's face, with thick blonde hair and a couture uniform of emerald-green, accenting her curves and matching her eyes. Emily's jealous side would have hated her immediately if her smile weren't so welcoming.

Emily caught her hand reaching subconsciously for the gold pendant on her new necklace, and redirected it before anyone noticed. Standing and straining to reach a full 5'5" height, she threw her shoulders back and chest out while holding her chin high. Then she directed her sandaled feet up the airstairs.

"Hello, Emily. I'm Alexandra. I'll be taking care of you this afternoon. Please, take any seat you'd like. Captain Roberts will have us in the air momentarily."

Emily looked around, drinking the atmosphere in. She'd never flown first class, much less private. Thick carpet of burnt gold, bird's-eye maple tables, and buttery-leather armchairs the color of crème caramel. The wall accents had been polished to a mirror shine, and the leather still smelled new. *Wow!*

She picked the second seat on the left side of the plane and sat with her face to the window. She resolved to sit that way until her face was as composed as Alexandra's.

Her mind was still racing in a dozen different directions.

She tried to let the rhythmic house music emanating from a dozen hidden speakers sweep her away while she watched a matched pair of white Rolls Royces disgorging a large family of Arabs near the airstair of a neighboring jet.

This really was happening.

If ever there was a time to call Jen, this was it. Surely there was a phone on the plane. If only she could remember Jen's number.

She turned from the window to find Alexandra standing there with a glass of champagne. "Captain Roberts said the control tower has delayed our departure, so we can get started."

Emily accepted the glass and immediately took a long sip, feeling the cool liquid slide all the way down. "Get started with what?"

Alexandra beckoned with her head in answer, and began walking toward the back of the plane. Her hips swayed in a fashion that even Emily found hypnotic. Some women were blessed top and bottom, front and behind.

Emily followed her to where the main cabin ended at a bird's-eye maple door in a matching wall. Alexandra pressed a button, and the door slid to the left, revealing a washroom far more spectacular than the one in her flat.

Emily's eyes immediately went to a blue and gold silk dress that popped from the glistening white surroundings like a flower from the desert sand. Then her eyes dropped to the floor beneath, where beautiful gold sandals and a matching purse waited. Emily looked back at Alexandra who nodded the affirmative.

An alarm tinkled in the back of her mind as she held the dress against her body and appraised the fit in the mirror. Perfect. She checked the shoes. Size seven. "How did Andreas know my sizes?"

Alexandra smiled. "He didn't. I sized you up during boarding. I've got eleven more dresses and five more pairs of shoes in a wardrobe up front."

"Is this some kind of uniform? Does Andreas do this every weekend?"

"Heavens no. It's Hermes. They don't do uniforms. I bought them while Michael was fetching you. I had a picture of the necklace to match, and your online profile to size with. Of course people tend to tell white lies online, so I allowed for variance. But you come exactly as advertised. Andreas assured me you would."

Alexandra paused for a moment. "As to your second question, the answer is *no*. To my knowledge, Andreas has never done this before."

Chapter 6

Alone

I SHOOK MY HEAD as the timbre of the jet's engines changed, and the Mediterranean Sea came into view on the horizon. "Tell me you got someone, Oscar. We're running out of time."

"It's coming in now," Oscar said. "Hold on."

Despite the radical shift our surveillance operation took when it suddenly went international, we'd reestablished our tactical advantage with a bit of subterfuge and a government G150 jet. By working with the control tower to learn Emily's flight schedule and then delay her departure, I was now following her plane from a hundred miles in front. Even The Ghost would be unlikely to spot me there. People look in their rearview mirrors for tails, not their windshields.

Our advantage would evaporate without a skilled and knowledgeable driver on the ground.

Getting a local agent to meet me shouldn't have been a problem, but for some reason, it was today. If Oscar didn't have a name soon, I'd either have to steal a car, or use a taxi to tail the most elusive criminal in modern history through the packed streets of Nice.

"Agent Joe Monfort will meet you at the plane."

"Hallelujah. What's his background?"

"It doesn't say anything."

Was this guy twelve, or did he think I was? "Don't bullshit me, Oscar. If it doesn't say anything, I'm sure you can look him up in the database. Tell me he's not a rookie. The last time you were vague about a partner, it turned out to be his first day in the field. This is no time for a training exercise."

"Half of OPEC is in Monaco for the Yacht Show. It's probably the single biggest gathering of Islamic billionaires in the world. The only reason you're getting anybody at all is because Director Rider personally made a call. By the way, he wanted me to remind you how important this operation is."

Of course he did. I was sure that deep down Oscar was aware of the contradictions coming out of his mouth, but on the surface he was clearly comfortable ignoring them. "Do we know his background? Tell me it's Special Forces or DGSE or DGSI, and not the Foreign Legion."

The CIA's Special Operations Group typically drafted veterans of other elite forces. The DGSE and DGSI were France's version of the CIA and FBI, and along with the COS, France's Special Operations Group, they were our favored recruiting grounds. Unfortunately France's top people typically preferred to stay domestic. The French Foreign Legion, on the other hand, was essentially a tough band of misfits who tended to be much bigger on brawn than intellect. Good horses, and much easier to recruit, but not the best for the course I was running. I wasn't sure if that was it, but I could tell Oscar was hiding something.

"You know what I know," Oscar said. "Regardless of background, I'm sure Joe can drive. What else do you need?"

I didn't have time to explain field operations to someone daft enough to ask that question. "Nothing."

"Good. Don't fuck up."

"How's the facial recognition coming?" By walking around the lobby of Palace Place while pretending to talk on my cell, I'd gotten decent video of Michael escorting Emily to the limo.

"Nothing yet. I checked with Willis, and he said it's clear that Michael's had facial surgery, so I'm not holding my breath." Willis was a plastic surgeon with the Department of Justice. The Witness Protection Program was his main gig, but he also consulted for the CIA.

"Great. How about the plane? Anything on it yet?" Emily's jet had a VP-C tail number, which I knew to be a Cayman Island registration. Not a good sign as far as transparency was concerned.

"It's a nested corporate registration, a regular onion. The owner went to great lengths to conceal its identity, which isn't that uncommon, as you know."

I did know. People who could afford to fly private tended to love their privacy as much as their lawyers loved all the billable hours they got to spend on the obfuscation. "Let me know the minute you've got it peeled."

The descent into Nice Cote D'Azur Airport was spectacular enough to lighten my mood, if only for a minute. Approaching over the red-tiled roofs of the French Riviera's exquisite mansions as we flew toward the Mediterranean's winking blue waters and sparkling white sands, I found myself enjoying my first lifestyles-of-the-rich-and-famous moment. Granted, my private jet was owned by the government, and I had been sent to dispatch an enemy of the state, but this was definitely a rosebud-worth-gathering moment, so to speak.

The CIA's Special Operations Group was the real-life version of the IMF, the fictional organization made famous in the Mission Impossible series. We had access to private jets, and some pretty cool equipment, although it was nowhere near the extravagant assortment Hollywood produced. The aspect that did match the show, however, was the requirement to operate under the radar.

I carried no special ID, wore no uniform, and used no equipment uniquely traceable to Uncle Sam. I also couldn't interact with foreign officials, even law enforcement — or get a better table at Spago.

Without the ability to turn to the locals for help, I really did need a competent French partner on the ground. It wasn't just a question of transportation. One never knew what would come up that might require local influence or expertise. Speaking of things coming at me, it appeared that Joe hadn't. I was looking at nothing but an empty carpet at the bottom of the G150's airstair.

Chapter 7

Transformation

AS HER PRIVATE JET soared over the gleaming waters of the English Channel, Emily found herself eager to learn everything Alexandra knew about her virtual boyfriend. "Do you work full-time for Andreas?"

Alexandra shook her head in a practiced manner that tossed her curls without being overtly flamboyant. "No, I work for an acquaintance of his. The man who owns the plane. He needed Andreas to stay the weekend, and offered this accommodation when Andreas explained his conflicting commitment to you."

"Sounds like a good acquaintance to have," Emily said. She was also dying to know where they were headed, but would have felt silly asking at that point, so instead she said, "How long is the flight?"

"About two hours," Alexandra said. "You can go back and change now. Take a shower if you'd like, but don't be too long. We'll need time for your mani-pedi, makeover, and hair."

Time for a mani-pedi, makeover, and hair. Of course. She wondered if she should ask someone to pinch her.

Emily had to take a shower if for no other reason than to take one on a plane. A private jet, no less. Heading to meet her new boyfriend somewhere on the continent for a dinner date. Unbelievable.

People always said she had pretty eyes. And she maintained a diet that held far more no's than yeses. She also worked hard to keep in shape with yoga and jogging. But she was no model. No Alexandra. Far from it.

She'd just found her soul mate, at long last.

And he happened to be rich.

After fumbling unsuccessfully with the clasp of her new necklace, she decided to leave it on, unwilling to risk jinxing things. While she lathered up with lilac-scented soap, Emily thought about the salon treatment to come. She silently promised herself that however this day turned out, she wouldn't get upset.

A couple of hours ago she'd been in the pit of despair, standing in her doorway with a broken phone and a wounded heart. Now she was living a life beyond her wildest dream. Even if Andreas turned out to be a fat old cretin who thought of women as objects of amusement, it would still be a day she could revisit. A story she could regale for the rest of her life.

That was a lie, of course.

If Andreas disappointed her, she'd be curled up in

the corner with a case of wine and a tear-soaked blanket until her fortieth birthday. Even Jen would stop calling. *Please, God. Please.*

"How well do you know Andreas?" she asked, picking up their earlier conversation, as Alexandra worked on her nails.

"We've never actually met. We just spoke on the phone."

"Oh?" Emily said, disappointed.

"He sure seemed smitten with you, though. He was much more interested in the details than most men, particularly the cut of your dress."

Emily looked down. The open front put her new necklace on prominent display, and more importantly, it did right by her cleavage. It wasn't a bad picture, a golden sun rising from a sea of blue silk between two mountains. Well, hills really, or hillocks perhaps. Regardless, in the abstract it resembled one of widow Cooper's paintings. Classy, if not sexy.

"It was a first for me," Alexandra continued. "Shopping for clothes for a woman my client had never seen. If you don't mind my asking, how did you and Andreas become acquainted?"

"We met through an online dating service, a couple of months ago."

"A couple of months? And you still haven't met in person?"

"Bad prior experiences made us both cautious. But

nonetheless, we soon developed an amazing online rapport. I felt as though he was inside my head. At some point I think we both became hesitant to meet because we didn't want to risk ruining the virtual relationship. We picked this date a month ago to take the pressure off, agreeing to meet if things were still going well. We didn't even set the details, just the time and place: my flat at 6:00 tonight."

"Not a restaurant?"

Emily tried replicating Alexandra's perky head shake. "We'd both been in situations where a date didn't show at a restaurant. So we agreed to meet out front of my building instead. If he didn't show, or I didn't come downstairs, then at least the other's embarrassment wouldn't be public."

"But still, giving out your address. Wasn't that risky?"

Emily thought about her secret. Was there any reason to keep it, given what she'd learned today? Quite the opposite, it seemed.

Sensing her hesitation, Alexandra kept talking. "I'm going to fix your hair up, if that's all right. Andreas mentioned that he loved the lines of your neck."

"I'm in your hands. To answer your question, I wanted Andreas to have my address. I wanted him to know that I live modestly."

Alexandra cocked her head. "I don't follow, but maybe that's because I spend my days helping the wealthy to look positively rich."

"My father is an influential public figure, a Member of Parliament. We don't communicate — we haven't since my mother died — but our estrangement is kept quiet for political reasons. His position is not a big deal, other than when it comes to my love life. For years now, most of the men I've dated have turned out to be more interested in my father than in me. That got a lot worse a year ago when he declared his candidacy in the London mayoral race."

Alexandra raised her eyebrows, and then began a delicate nod. "So you began hiding your true identity, and removed any connection to status from your profile. And your modest flat does nothing to break the illusion. I guess I can see the logic in that. If you don't mind my asking, what is your family name?"

"Aspinwall. I'm Emily Aspinwall."

Alexandra's pupil's flared. "I don't follow politics, but that's still a name I recognize. Your father's leading in the polls."

Emily nodded.

"That must be exciting. Does the Mayor of London get a jet?"

"I have no idea. If he does, I'll never see it. But in any case, I'm sure that if you're the Mayor of London, there are plenty of people willing to lend you theirs."

"No doubt about that. Eighty percent of the miles on this plane are logged for favors. Gives my boss a hefty sack of IOU's."

And now one of them has Andreas's name on it, Emily thought. "You're not looking to change employers, are you? Looks to me like you've got it pretty good."

"I do. But I think I'd rather have a British boss."

"Who's your boss now?"

"Like me, he's Russian."

"Really? You don't have an accent."

A mischievous look crossed Alexandra's face. "I've worked hard."

"We're not headed for Moscow, are we?"

"Michael didn't tell you where we're going?"

"He seems to have a predilection for the mysterious."

Alexandra seemed to have a penchant for suspense herself. "Stand up and look at yourself in the mirror," she said.

They walked back to the bathroom where Emily admired the total transformation that Alexandra had wrought. She'd never looked better. Perfect hair, a fashionable dress, a flawless mani-pedi, and an exquisite gold necklace. If only she'd met Alexandra the day of her ten-year high school reunion. "You're a miracle worker."

"You made it easy. You've got great bone structure. But I must say, I'm pleased with the result. Which is a good thing, because it would be a shame to have you looking anything but your very best … at the Monaco Yacht Show."

Chapter 8

Follow the Money

I WAS ABOUT to get Oscar back on the line when a crotch-rocket roared in and screeched to a halt. It was a beautiful machine, a black Kawasaki Ninja with neon-green highlights. When the young driver removed her matching helmet and shook out her long brown hair, I saw that she was beautiful too. I could hear Oscar laughing all the way from Virginia.

"Achilles, I presume. I'm Jo Monfort."

Granger had trained me to act and react quickly and fluidly, so when Jo-without-the-*e* tossed me a helmet, I caught it with a smile.

This was far from the situation I'd been expecting, which involved an SUV loaded with equipment and a driver who could take down a whole bar without removing the cigarette pursed between his lips. At least I could be certain she wasn't former Foreign Legion. "Pleasure to meet you, Jo. Nice bike."

"You'll be glad we have it. Traffic is horrible this

time of year, and parking is worse. Much better to tail someone on two wheels than four."

I was tempted to ask if she was speaking from experience or just textbooks, but simply said, "Good idea."

Jo wore black leather boots and pants, topped with a gray leather jacket that was more runway than roadway, tilting her overall look toward fashionable. It was a versatile outfit, a good choice. The ash-gray color matched her eyes, which hinted at a fire within. "Thanks."

She handed me an earpiece. "We'll be able to talk using these. Hop on. Emily's plane is on approach."

I already had an earpiece linking me to Oscar. I considered swapping it with Jo's, but ended up sticking hers in my left ear instead. I needed to monitor both.

It was starting to get crowded in my head.

I'd ridden plenty of sport bikes over the years, but never on the back. The rear seat rose about four inches above the driver's, which combined with the seven or so I had on Jo, put my head above hers like a totem pole. My arms were long enough that I could have easily grabbed the handlebars as well, but that would be dangerous. I had to hold on to Jo instead.

Tethering a two hundred twenty pound weight to a hundred and twenty pound post didn't make a lot of sense. Neither did placing the bike's center of gravity so far back. The short drive to Jo's selected observation point was enough to make that obvious. She hit the kickstand and said, "You should sit up front."

"The physics do appear to favor that arrangement."

As we switched, Emily's plane taxied into its disembarkation position near the VIP parking lot.

"I've got a monocular in the left pannier if you want it," Jo said.

"Thanks. What else you got in there?"

"A couple of suppressed Glocks, some flash-bangs, a lock-picking gun, a directional microphone, and a Range-R radar system."

Range-R radar looks through walls like X-rays through flesh. Very cool. The new unit looked like a heavy-duty smartphone, and was a literal lifesaver in breaching situations — for the good guys. The bad guys, not so much. "They gave you the latest goodies."

"We do tend to keep up with fashion here, if nothing else. What's our mission?"

"What did they tell you?"

"Just that we're following the passengers of a private jet in hopes that they'll lead us to a high-value target. Also that Director Rider is personally watching this one, so it's make it or break it for my career."

Jo was modest and direct. My opinion of her was growing by the minute. "What were you doing before the CIA approached you?"

"Long story. Who's the target?"

"Ivan the Ghost."

"Who?"

If Jo didn't know Ivan, she wasn't former DGSE or DGSI. In fact, she wasn't coming from any law enforcement agency in the northern hemisphere. "He's the guy you go to when you need dirty deeds done discreetly, and you've got seven figures to pay for it. We think he's Russian, thus *Ivan*, but we're not even sure of that. No one ever sees him coming and he never leaves a trace, thus *The Ghost*."

"Until now, I gather."

"Exactly."

"Which is why the Director is involved."

"It would be a huge win for him right out of the gate."

"I understand," she replied, with an inflection that told me she was familiar with Rider's political situation. "Why haven't I heard of Ivan the Ghost before this?"

"He leaves neither trail nor trace that couldn't be explained away by bad luck and circumstance. With no evidence, only the tabloid presses run stories on him, and those are next to Bigfoot and alien babies.

"The only credible people who know anything about him are the powerful victims he's embarrassed or the law enforcement officers he's bested, and they're not talking to the press, for obvious reasons. Plenty of people in law enforcement believe he's no more real than the Loch Ness Monster. They think he's just a convenient excuse, a coverall explanation for the unexplained. And to their point, there is no evidence of his existence that goes beyond the circumstantial."

"So how did you end up on his tail?"

"Director Rider discovered that one of the two leading candidates in the London mayoral race made a seven-figure payment to an account previously used by The Ghost. We assume it was a contract payment, and that the contract was to discreetly eliminate his chief rival for the office. So we've been watching the rival's pressure points. The girl on the plane is his daughter."

As I gave Jo more background on Ivan and our mission, the airstair from Emily's Falcon 5X dropped and Michael descended, followed by a woman in a blue and gold silk dress.

"Is that Emily?" Jo asked.

I used the monocular to be sure. "That's her. Unfortunately, they swapped out the purse I'd tagged with a cricket. They also gave her a new wardrobe and full makeover at 30,000 feet. Her head must be reeling. A few hours ago she was just expecting dinner."

"Why would they do all that?"

"If I were to speculate, I'd say that it's part of The Ghost's plan to leave no traces. Wherever she's headed, that's the look that will fit in."

As I brought the Ninja's engine roaring to life, Jo asked a question that convinced me she'd been a good recruit. "How'd the director get a lead on Ivan's bank account? I'd think The Ghost would change those as often as his socks."

"I don't know. That's been bothering me too. But you're right about Ivan. He would."

Chapter 9

Little Tells

EMILY BEGAN TO LAUGH as Michael pulled the Black Mercedes S550 up to the valet stand at the Monaco Yacht Show's VIP entrance. A flood of nervous tension had spontaneously decided to leave her body without pausing to ask permission.

"Miss?" Michael's quizzical eyes were focused on the rearview mirror.

Despite her embarrassment, she met his eyes. She liked Michael. "Three hours ago I was standing in The Regent's Park boating lake, holding onto hope and the remains of my broken phone. Now I'm here." She gestured with both arms. "It's almost literally unbelievable. Way too good to be true, as my friend Jen would say, and yet undeniable."

"I think you'll find yourself adapting quickly. The good things are like that."

Emily was sure Michael was right. It was the return to reality that concerned her, but again she promised herself to live for the moment while the moment was hers.

The next couple of minutes filled a mental scrapbook with photos, the new highlights of her lifetime. Her first step from the limo was onto the blue VIP carpet, complete with a gawking crowd wondering if she was famous, or just rich. Then there was the handsome guard in an immaculate white uniform, studying Michael's proffered credentials before ceremoniously parting the curtain to wonderland. Next came the sparkling chrome bannisters and glistening white bows of the latest crop of superyachts, each attempting to catch an appraising eye and then capture a burning checkbook.

"Is the show open to the public?" she asked Michael, as he led her through the pampered crowd along Port Hercules' southernmost pier.

"It's open to anyone willing to plop down a hundred and fifty euros for the privilege. They were expecting over thirty thousand visitors this year, with the economy recovering. I haven't heard how many actually showed."

"You talk as though it's over."

"The show formally ended at 6:30 this evening. This is the aftershow. With hoi polloi out of the way, the real players emerge, and the serious business gets done."

Emily wondered what qualified as *the masses* at the Monaco Yacht Show. *Was it anyone with less than seven figures in their checking account, or eight?*

With dusk approaching, the underwater lights on all of the yachts were illuminating, giving the sea an azure glow that complemented the orange horizon. It was nothing short of magical and a perfect time for pictures.

If only she had her phone.

Glancing behind as she tried to take it all in, Emily saw that the residents on the balconies adorning every square meter of real estate on the streets and cliffs above had the same idea. The privileged onlookers were drinking cocktails and taking selfies while reveling in one of the most spectacular combinations of natural and manmade beauty on Earth.

She read off the names of the superyachts they passed, pleased to make their acquaintance. *Thumper*, *Perseus*, *4 You*, *Flying Dragon* — each illuminated like an exclusive club or five-star restaurant. Each representing a special place, a secret world, a life as different from the one she knew as the land was from the sea. While she marveled at the sight of luxury speedboats docked inside the belly garage of the nearest colossus, a thought struck her like a cold splash of ocean spray. How could she possibly fit into Andreas's world?

Their whirlwind online romance had uncovered the things she thought were important, the little tells that revealed his soul. She knew that Andreas was raised Catholic, read poetry when depressed, and became a vegetarian at age fourteen while volunteering at an animal shelter. She knew that he'd studied philosophy at the Sorbonne before earning a graduate degree from the London School of Economics. She knew that he had a niche consulting business that took him all over the world. And she knew that he collected refrigerator magnets wherever he went, although she hadn't given any thought to the extravagance of the room his refrigerator might be in.

They were only about midway along the Rainier III dock, but Emily realized that there was only one gangplank remaining ahead. The attached yacht looked to be about twice the size of Palace Place.

She stopped dead in her tracks.

"You're kidding?"

Michael halted as well and turned to her with a smile. "At 110 meters, the *Anzhelika* is one of the largest, and of course most expensive in the world."

"Do I even want to know?"

"Over a quarter-billion euros, I believe."

"Who's Anzhelika?"

"The owner's mother."

Emily wondered if the christening made his mother proud, or ashamed. She didn't know how many schools or clinics could be operated with a quarter-billion dollar endowment, but her assumption was that it was double digits in most countries, and triple in some. Maybe that was what Andreas was doing here — seeking a donation for a worthy cause.

"You okay?" Michael asked.

"Just a bit overwhelmed."

"I understand. Do you need a minute to collect yourself before meeting Andreas?"

Her emotional overload had led to laughter a few minutes earlier. Now she was afraid that tears would start streaming if she didn't keep moving. "No, I'm fine."

Michael put an arm on her shoulder. "Everyone on that yacht does the same things you do, and feels the same things you feel, eighty percent of the time. Keep that perspective in mind while you enjoy this twenty percent situation."

His words of wisdom struck home. "Thank you. Tell me, how long have you been with Andreas?"

He grew a wry smile. "From the beginning."

The beginning of what? she wondered. Michael was only about forty — too young to have been with Andreas since birth. In a servant's capacity at least. Maybe he was the son of Andreas's father's butler, or something like that. Maybe Michael really was Andreas, and this was all an act to give him a peek behind her facades and defenses. She'd know soon enough.

Two large men whose disposition seemed more soldierly than cordial gave Michael a nod and stepped away from the foot of the *Anzhelika's* gangplank. *Were those sidearms under their pressed white jackets?*

"After you," Michael said.

Chapter 10

Choices

THE VIP GATE ATTENDANT, a GQ/Soldier hybrid in a pressed white suit, gave me a look that indicated he didn't think I was VI. "Sorry, sir, but the show closed at 6:30. With the prince making the rounds, only owners and their guests are allowed in this evening. You can't get in without an invitation. And you can't leave your motorbike here."

As I pulled out my wallet, he nodded toward an overhead camera. "Don't bother, sir. Along with the Grand Prix, this is our signature event. The principality takes security very seriously."

With every second of delay, Emily was disappearing deeper into the crowd. And since they'd swapped out her purse, I had no electronic means of tracking her.

I ran back to the Ninja, and Jo. "Are there other entrances, or do I need to get more creative?"

Jo pointed. "Around the corner and down a hundred meters or so. Aren't you glad I brought the bike?"

"Yes. You're a genius."

We covered the distance in about a second and a half, after which I backed the Ninja in between a shiny black Maserati and an equally polished white panel van. I slipped the Range-R into a breast pocket opposite my Glock, while Jo stuffed a few items into her purse before locking the pannier. "This event has vendors, right?" I asked. "Companies selling yachts and navigation systems and jewelry for the mistress?"

"Of course. Hundreds."

"Do you know what admission costs?"

"At least a hundred euros, I'd guess. But they're not selling tickets tonight."

"They're always selling tickets. It's just a question of tactics and price."

"Tactics and price?"

"A price that motivates flexibility, and tactics that supply an excuse to bend."

I kept simple tools with me at all times, including paperclips, parachute cord, and bills of large denomination. I palmed five hundred euros, leading Jo toward the gate and scoping the scene as we walked. I angled our approach to put my back in the right place while we passed the guard, and strode toward him exuding authority like the chief of police.

Jo followed suit.

This guard appeared to be the other guy's twin — a model's face with a soldier's physique and grooming.

The Prince of Monaco's version of a corporate receptionist. He eyed us with interest, but not alarm. "We left our badges back at the Rolex booth. They just gave us this temporary pass." I slipped the bill into his left palm without breaking stride, leaving him with two options.

He made the wrong choice.

He grabbed my right shoulder with his right hand.

Throughout history, the Latin proverb *"Fortune Favors the Bold"* has been adopted as the motto of many of the world's elite military forces, urging soldiers to undertake the same valiant action that helped create the Roman Empire. It's a tactic I often employ, both because it's a personality fit, and because most people are content to leave well enough alone.

Unfortunately, this guy wasn't.

By grabbing my shoulder, he'd invoked another classic axiom: Newton's Third Law of Motion.

I shot my left hand up and clamped it down above his right, trapping it atop my shoulder while lifting my right elbow and spinning around in a rapid, fluid sequence. This combination placed the startled guard into an arm lock that forced his face down and set his head up like a football on a kicking tee. He'd miscalculated, inviting a world of hurt, and now all he could do was suck it up and take it.

The key to a knockout blow is overwhelming the central nervous system and effectively tripping a circuit breaker. Boxers do this by delivering a jaw strike powerful enough that the brain not only smacks into the back of the skull, but also recoils forward to concuss the front, creating a two-pronged neural attack. I was no heavyweight boxer, but I was using a knee rather than a fist, which was like upgrading from .22 to .45 caliber ammunition. And my cross-country skier thighs packed a magnum load.

The sound told me I'd gotten it just right, a clean crack reminiscent of a home run baseball swing. The effect was as stark and immediate as flipping a light switch. He went from rigid to limp in a millisecond.

I caught him and dumped him back behind his little podium while Jo looked on with wide eyes.

"You were saying something about tactics and price?" she said.

I shrugged. "He didn't like my tactics, and so he paid the price."

"Will he be okay?"

"He'll be fine. Five hundred euros buys a lot of aspirin. Unfortunately, we're now marked if anyone was watching. Let's move."

We headed back toward the VIP gate, hoping to get lucky and spot Emily right away. Without prompting, Jo split off to my left, helping us better blend into the crowd. Her instincts were solid.

The blue-carpeted dock was lined with pristine white vendor tents on one side, and envy-provoking yachts on the other. I hand-signaled Jo that we should divide our attention, with her scanning the yachts while I checked the booths.

My eyes still roving, I got Oscar back on the mike.

"Where are you?" Oscar asked.

I ignored his question and asked one of my own. "Who owns the jet?"

"They're peeling back the last layer of the onion now. Hold on. How are things on your end?"

"We're at the Monaco Yacht Show. We lost them at the VIP entrance — no tickets — but are inside now attempting reacquisition."

"You better do more than attempt, Achilles. Failure is not an option."

Failure is not an option. Anyone who said that had never been in a firefight. You learned pretty fast when bullets were flying that failure was always an option. A bit of bad luck with a ricochet, or a weapons malfunction, put failure front and center. But I wasn't about to fail.

We were scanning the busy crowd with the intensity of desperation as we walked in the direction of the VIP gate. Michael had shed half his chauffeur's uniform in the Mercedes, and emerged wearing just a white shirt and black slacks. Dressed that way, he matched half the male crowd. But with his broad shoulders and 6' frame, I still hoped to spot him quickly.

Emily, now about 5'8" with heels on and hair up,

was wearing blue and gold silk. The dress would make her an easy mark in most crowds, but not this one. Blue and gold were nautical colors, and silk dresses more plentiful during cocktail hour in Monaco than either shorts or jeans.

"Got it," Oscar said. "Arman Voskerchyan owns the jet. Know the name?"

"Russia's wealthiest citizen, according to Forbes, although I'm sure his actual wealth pales in comparison to President Korovin's. Is it his jet?" *Of course it was*, I thought. That made perfect sense.

"It is."

"I'm sure he owns a yacht or six. Are any of them at the Monaco Yacht Show?"

"If his boat registrations are nested like his aircraft, it's going to take a while to build a query. Voskerchyan controls over a hundred corporations, and they're registered all over the world, from Shanghai to Lagos to St. Kitts."

"NASA allegedly spent ten million dollars to develop a ballpoint pen that would write in space. Know what the Russian Space Program did?"

"Paid a NASA engineer a thousand bucks for the plans?"

"They used a pencil."

"What's your point?"

"Google it. The Monaco Yacht Show is a prestige event, and those run on publicity."

Oscar didn't respond right away, but he came back in under a minute. "The *Anzhelika*. It measures at 110 meters. When it launched it was the second most expensive yacht in the world."

We were back in business. Relief flooded over me until I thought about our next move in context. A Russian oligarch could pack a small army of security guards onto a yacht of the *Anzhelika's* size.

Chapter 11

High Society

EMILY'S FEET barely touched the gangplank as she boarded. First the limo, then the jet, and now this unbelievable yacht. Her life would never be the same now that she had enjoyed the equivalent of fifteen minutes of fame.

And the night was still young.

The *Anzhelika's* main lobby was dominated by a grand circular staircase, running both up and down. A master craftsman had carved dolphins and octopi and schools of tropical fish into the banisters and rails with such precision that she half expected them to swim. Michael passed the sculpture by without a glance, leading her through an open double doorway above which was written *main saloon*.

The decorator had paneled this grand room with cherry wood, and furnished it with armchairs and custom-shaped couches and piles of pillows — all upholstered from rich Italian brocades the color of cotton, hummus, and gold.

Tonight, the owner had filled it with pampered guests, all dressed to the nines and drinking fine wines, while conversing in a panoply of languages. Emily detected English, French, Chinese, Arabic, and Russian. A veritable United Nations, but far more upbeat and harmonious than the typical General Assembly, she suspected.

"We're right on time," Michael said. "Andreas told me he'd be out on the aft deck. Would you like me to show you, or can you find your way?"

"I'd appreciate an escort," Emily said, not entirely sure she'd be able to pick Andreas out of the crowd. She'd only seen his blurry profile picture, and as Jen loved to point out, those tended to be lies of height and weight and follicular status. Given the omission of his economic status, or at least that of his friends, she was prepared for a large pendulum swing — in the less attractive direction.

Andreas's appearance really didn't matter to her, so long as his age was in the same ballpark, and his sentiments had been genuine.

And they had been.

Jen had asserted her skeptical manner, and together they'd verified the history of her dialogue with Andreas. That check confirmed it. When it came to likes and dislikes and social opinions, Andreas had led. He'd spoken first. He hadn't been telling her what he knew she wanted to hear, because he had no information from her to follow.

Maybe he was like Stephen Hawking or something — brilliant and sensitive but seriously handicapped? Maybe he was a dwarf? Maybe he was pushing eighty?

She studied the crowd as they crossed the saloon, her eyes naturally gravitating to the other women — to their figures, their jewelry, and their dresses. They were clustered in fours or fives, each homogenous in their composition and choice of beverage. White wine or mixed drinks for the older cliques. Champagne or sparkling water for the younger.

All the women were beautiful.

Going by faces and figures, there wasn't a woman over thirty-nine in the room. Judging by necks and hands, about half were north of fifty. Those were the wives, Emily figured. The rest were mid to late twenties, like her. Except not. The girlfriends clearly skipped both lunch and dinner in favor of the gym, and then spent their evenings either strutting elite Italian runways, or working exclusive Paris clubs.

The men were of two sorts as well. There were the masters of the universe, with their Cognac and cigars, scattered about in groups of two to four, and there were security guards — solo figures blending into corners, with thick necks, watchful eyes, and ear mikes. Emily supposed that made sense. There was probably as much jewelry on the *Anzhelika* as in the Tower of London.

They crossed onto the aft deck and into the open air, where she found more of the same. Emily's eyes darted between the male guests, attempting to locate Andreas. She found it an odd experience, looking for someone whose soul she knew but whose face she had yet to experience.

When her first pass failed to produce a fitting candidate, she turned to Michael.

He too looked perplexed. "He's not here. Let's try the next level up. Technically speaking, there are five aft decks."

"How many decks does the *Anzhelika* have?"

"Six. The two below us are service levels, containing engineering, the galley, the tender boats, and the crew quarters. He wouldn't be on either of those. The three above are all candidates."

They took an external staircase to the fourth level. Michael paused at the top, hesitant to intrude. They surveyed the scene from the shadows. It was reminiscent of the one below, but smaller and less populated. "This is the owner's deck," Michael said. "I see the owner, but not Andreas."

"Is he the tan gentleman in blue slacks and a white jacket?"

"You'd think, wouldn't you? But no, that's the Chairman of DeBeers."

"The diamond company."

"Yep. Mister Voskerchyan is the man he's speaking

with."

Emily studied her host from behind. He was small but stocky, like a wrestler. Well into his fifties by her estimation, his hair was still thick and naturally black. He wore black slacks and loafers. A fitted black sweater with the sleeves pushed up onto forearms broader than her calves completed the look. She couldn't see his face, but from behind, the adjective Voskerchyan's appearance brought to mind was *tough*.

"Let's try the next," Michael said.

The aft deck on five had but one couple — a younger man and woman busy getting to know each other's dental work. Michael didn't even pause. He kept right on climbing.

The aft portion of the top deck was circular rather than oblong like the rest, and for good reason. It was a helipad, complete with a big silver bird. Unable to help herself, Emily blurted out, "Wow!"

Michael said, "It's nice, but it's not Mister Voskerchyan's toy of choice this year."

Emily looked around, wondering what could be more fantastic.

"It's not up here," Michael said. "It's down on deck one. Care to guess?"

She pictured the speedboats she'd seen earlier, and let her imagination run with it. "A jet boat? A hovercraft?"

A third voice answered correctly. "A new

submarine."

They turned toward it and Emily saw a man in black slacks and a black shirt walking in their direction. He was above average in height and athletic in build. A spring in his step spoke of pent-up energy. His smile showed teeth, and his eyes showed fire. And his hair showed that he worked hard to look like his appearance didn't matter. The resemblance to his picture was only slight. Live, he looked much better.

Michael said, "Emily, allow me to introduce Andreas."

Chapter 12

The Split

ANZHELIKA WAS ENORMOUS. One hundred and ten meters was the length of a football field, including both end zones. It would be easy to find, even in this superyacht crowd. Searching it, on the other hand, was going to be a challenge. And before we could search it, we had to get aboard.

"It's in the berth closest to open water at the far end of the Rainier III dock, which is at the southern end of Port Hercules," Oscar said.

"Makes sense. Probably the only place a monster like that would fit. Send me the deck plan."

"How are you going to get aboard?"

"I don't know yet."

"Well you need to figure it out fast. I don't want to have to swoop back in and save your ass again. The Director just reminded me that this is his top priority. You hear that, Achilles? Nothing is more important to the CIA on this day than catching Ivan. Nothing."

"You don't need to remind me."

"Good. Then stop talking, and start doing."

I'd read that Steve Jobs was a real prick, but people lined up to work for him because he was such a genius. Well, Oscar was no genius.

There was a sizable gaggle and a lot of hubbub coming our way along the dock, including a TV camera and a boom mike. A trio of sailors was out front like the head of a spear, firmly but gracefully clearing the way.

"We're in luck," Jo said, over her mike. "Here comes the prince."

I wasn't sure that was lucky. If an alert had gone out after our little incident at the gate, the prince's security would surely have it.

I watched Jo size up each member of the entourage as though she had something in mind. We'd spread apart earlier to avoid looking like a couple in case there was a BOLO alert, but once her royal recce was complete she moved back to my side. I wasn't sure what she was up to, but something about the look in her eye made me willing, even eager, to play along.

Still watching the oncoming procession, she began to talk with animation, gesticulating left and right out of context. "Did they tell you how I came to S-O-G?"

"No. They didn't tell me anything. Not even your full name."

"It's Josephine, like Napoleon's love. When I was born I think my parents had plans for me that were far above their station. But they never called me anything but Jo, so that's who I've always been. Anyway, from the time I could walk, if I wasn't in school I helped out with the family business."

"Which was?"

"We ran sophisticated confidence scams. Relieved those with too much money of some of their burden. Long story short, a year ago I ended up, quite by accident, with the briefcase and wallet of the US Ambassador to France."

"You what?"

The gaggle was just a few feet from us now, and Jo spun about and began walking backwards so that she could face me while she talked, all the while continuing with her wild gesticulations. "It was a dangerous situation for me, and an embarrassing situation for His Excellency. You know, if there's one thing you learn growing up with con artists, it's how to look at a situation from different angles. I chose to look at that situation as an opportunity to switch professions." Jo spun back around, colliding as she did so with a younger man near the rear of the prince's entourage. It was a full-on collision, causing them both to tumble like drunken dancers into the woman he'd been speaking with.

Jo began apologizing immediately and rapidly in French, trying to comfort the victims of her carelessness, while she steadied them like a pair of floor vases she'd caused to totter. *She was so clumsy. So stupid. So sorry.*

The procession moved on without notice. All eyes still riveted to the prince. All ears straining to hear his witty reflections on this year's event.

Jo returned to my side and continued walking as though nothing had happened. After a few steps she pressed something into my hand, holding it for a moment for appearances' sake.

I shifted my grip to check her pulse. Slow and steady.

Using a feigned wipe of my brow to check the contents of my palm, I said, "You may be new to S-O-G, but you're no stranger to the field."

Jo had passed me a small stack of business cards. They were embossed with the coat of arms of Monaco and bore the vague but powerful title, *Office of His Highness, Prince Albert II of Monaco.* No doubt she'd scored the woman's card for herself. "Very nice. What's your title?"

"Secretary to His Highness."

"You reckon these are our tickets to the party?"

"I do reckon."

We were still a half-kilometer from *Anzhelika.* The sun was setting and the dock was clearing, but the yachts were coming to life as champagne corks were popped and cigars were lit and deals were inked. "Are you going to finish your story?" I asked Jo.

"Can't you guess the rest?"

"I doubt my guessing would have the flamboyance of your telling."

"I found my way into the ambassador's residence and left the briefcase and wallet under his pillow."

"With a card, I assume?"

"The alternative would have been rude."

"What did you write?"

"Please find my curriculum vitae attached. Yours respectfully, Josephine Monfort. Along with my phone number, of course."

"Of course."

I held up my hand and began tabulating with my fingers. "*Skills, balls, integrity, ingenuity,* and *cheek.* I could see Granger weighing that lineup on par with a chest full of combat ribbons."

She held up a hand and made the peace sign. "I noticed that you ran out of fingers before you got to *respect* and *lateral thinking.* They're very big on those at Langley."

"Those go without saying."

"It was Granger who evaluated me on the ambassador's recommendation, but he was gone before I completed my training. I liked him. Were the two of you close?"

"He brought me in, trained me, and functioned as my control for four years. He's a great man and a good friend."

"You obviously miss him. I only met Oscar briefly. He comes across as more of a politician."

"Let's just say he and Granger have different strengths."

"So what's your story? Special Forces?"

"No, I was also the oddball of my class."

"Do tell."

I didn't like talking about myself, but the *Anzhelika* was still a couple of minutes walk away, and there was nothing like casual conversation to help a couple blend in. Security would be looking for people exuding purpose. Jo seemed to intuit this. "I was a biathlete until a back injury ended my career."

"By biathlete, you mean shooting and skiing?"

"That's right."

"Were you any good?"

"I grew up in Colorado, where both are obsessions. I was obsessed enough to make the Olympic team."

"No kidding? Wow! How'd you do?"

"I won bronze in Vancouver. But of course I wanted gold. I was totally committed to winning it too, when I hurt my back."

"That sucks."

"It happens a lot. I didn't want to let it make me bitter, so I funneled all my energy into rock climbing, which is another Colorado obsession."

"The back injury didn't prevent that?"

"You'd think, but no. Different force vectors." This

was starting to feel more like a first date than an SOG op, and I found myself enjoying it. Apparently eight weeks of working exclusively with Oscar had left a void.

"Well, it seems to have worked. You don't strike me as bitter."

"Thanks. Actually, the Olympic disappointment made me reckless. Desperate to prove myself, I went straight for free-soloing, which is where you climb without ropes or equipment. I tackled cliffs like they were battlefields and I was my ancient namesake.

"With that attitude and my Olympic conditioning, I managed to set a couple of speed records. Nothing newsworthy anywhere outside Colorado or climbing circles, but enough to make the local papers. Granger was visiting the Air Force Academy, saw an article and got curious." I paused, recalling the events.

"He ended up recruiting me. Kinda made me his pet project and brought in some top guns for one-on-one training, since I didn't have the typical Special Forces background. I was very fortunate."

"How long ago was that?"

"Five years."

"I just finished up at The Farm five days ago. I'm barely over the jet lag."

"Well, you're doing fantastic so far. Those were great moves, by the way. I was looking for some sleight of hand, but still didn't see a thing."

"Merci beaucoup."

I grabbed Jo's arm and guided her into a vacant tent. "What is it?"

"Michael's coming down the *Anzhelika's* gangplank. He's dressed the same as when he left the Mercedes, but now he's carrying a large tan leather bag.

"Do you have a cricket?"

"Afraid not."

"Crap. Time for a tactical pivot. I think you should follow him while I go after Emily."

"Aren't you going to need my help searching the ship?"

"That would be nice, but finding Ivan is the mission and two links to him are better than one. We're operating as though Emily is on the *Anzhelika* and Ivan is with her, but those are both assumptions. One of us should stick with Michael until the other spots Ivan. And since he saw my face earlier today in London, it can't be me."

"Makes sense," Jo said, her voice a bit hesitant.

"Familiarize yourself with the way he moves. He's got a distinctive gait. Reminds me of a wrestler walking onto the mat. Recognizing it will make it easier to tail him if he employs counter-surveillance tactics. Under no circumstances are you to engage him, understood? He may appear to be a nice guy, but I know a carnivore when I see one."

"Okay."

"I mean it."

"I understand."

"We'll keep our mikes live, and regroup as soon as one of us has something. Agreed?"

I saw a trace of fear in Jo's eyes, but she said, "As you wish."

Chapter 13

Slippery Moves

JO FELT a drop of adrenaline hit her bloodstream as she took up Michael's tail. She'd followed hundreds of marks through the streets of Paris and Nice while running her scams, but this was different. This time she had a concealed weapon, and no doubt that her mark was lethally armed. A slick tongue and swift feet might prove insufficient if she slipped up and caught his eye.

With Achilles by her side, chasing Ivan the Ghost had felt like another training op, even though it was her first actual mission. Alone now, she understood that this was very different.

Another drop of adrenaline.

Port Hercules twinkled like a Christmas tree, with a hundred superyachts ornamenting the azure waters, all polished for show and festooned with lights. Twilight was a tough time to tail in any circumstances, with the setting sun and dancing shadows playing tricks on the eyes, but the perpetual motion and cascading contrasts of the Monaco Yacht Show magnified those effects exponentially.

As the partygoers came in and the exhibitors went out, rolling cases of equipment and bags of all sizes, Michael's distant form was bouncing in and out of focus with every other stride.

And then he simply wasn't there.

"Merde!"

She'd forgotten that Achilles was live in her ear, so when he responded, it was like the voice of God. "What's wrong?"

"Michael just disappeared."

"Just this second?"

"Yes."

"Keep walking as though nothing happened. The difference between tailing someone like Michael and one of your civilian marks is that he has been trained in countermeasures. His use of them doesn't necessarily mean he's spotted you. With time, countermeasures become reflexive. But this does indicate that his radar will be finely tuned, so whatever you do, don't stop and look around as though you've lost your puppy.

"How far back were you when it happened?"

"About thirty meters."

"Good. Keep walking while you search using your peripheral vision. Once you're about twenty meters past the point he disappeared, stop and pull out your smartphone. Lean against a post or something, someplace that gives you the right perspective. Keep your face pointed down towards your phone, scanning for him only with your eyes. Got it?"

"Got it."

"Good. Keep in mind that he might change his appearance. Everything is game — from his hair and clothes, to his apparent age and stride. If in doubt, check the pants and shoes. They're usually the last to go. Just remember what they taught you at The Farm and you'll do fine. You're clearly a natural."

"Thank you. Will do."

"I just talked my way onto the *Anzhelika* as advance security for the prince, using the card you so brilliantly procured. Now I need to keep a low profile, so talking will be problematic. If you don't reacquire Michael in the next ten minutes, join me here."

"Okay."

"And Jo, remember, whatever you do, don't engage this guy. He's too good. It's not worth it."

She wasn't going to let Michael outwit her. No way. Not on her first case. Not with Director Rider personally paying attention.

She'd last seen Michael before the big exhibition tent. Unlike the little ones lining the dock like dominoes, the big air-conditioned tent had many dozens of subdivisions for luxury vendors. To go in after him would be like entering a maze.

She could wait outside, but there were two exits,

spaced about sixty meters apart. Surveying both would be difficult, especially given the perspective required to see through disguises. On top of all that, she had to act fast.

She performed a quick 180-degree sweep, searching for a location that would make it possible to view both exits. Someplace that wouldn't draw attention while her head pivoted back and forth like a spectator at a tennis match.

Her eyes zoomed in on the upper decks of the flanking yachts near the middle of the row. Most were blazing with light and buzzing with activity, but *Victor's Secret* was relatively dark, and appeared quiet. Perhaps Victor was busy inspecting lingerie in the master's suite, but given the hour, she was hopeful that he was either dining at one of Monaco's many Michelin-starred restaurants, or living large at the Casino de Monte-Carlo.

Jo boarded the darkened yacht as if she owned it and looked for an external staircase that would take her to an upper deck without breaking her surveillance line of sight. There wasn't one.

She decided to climb.

A few basic gymnastics moves was all it would take, given the preponderance of rails. Child's play for a cat burglar who'd trained as a gymnast. *Former* cat burglar, she corrected herself.

Two kip casts, paired with neck kip to stand springs,

and she was three decks up on post — less than a minute after hanging up with Achilles.

"What are you doing?" The challenge had been issued from the dock. The speaker was a middle-aged passerby holding hands with a teenage wife.

"Shhh," she said, with a finger to her lips. "It's supposed to be a surprise."

The man grimaced as the woman yanked his hand. "Sorry," he mouthed.

Jo pulled out her monocular and began the back and forth sweep that would not stop until she'd either reacquired her target, or her ten minutes had expired. She used her naked left eye to take in the big picture, and then shifted to the scope on her right whenever somebody deserved a closer look. As she'd been trained, Jo ignored context. It didn't matter if the man was pushing a wheelchair or part of a crowd, if his build was the right proportion, he got her full scrutiny. Fortunately, with the show now closed, the mobs were gone. And as a bonus, most people exiting the big tent were hauling luggage that slowed their pace.

Jo wondered how Achilles was fairing on the *Anzhelika*. She enjoyed audacious moves like his. They'd been the hallmark of her previous profession. But she'd always kept to the shadows. Achilles had walked right past the gorillas into the lion's den. That was bold, and risky. Russian oligarchs weren't known to be charitable to their enemies.

Despite the odds, she was betting that her first partner would pull it off. There was an air about him, a combination of confidence and charisma that she found inspiring. Maybe that came with being an Olympian. She'd never met one before. In any case, she was determined not to let him down.

A couple of men, both the right age and size, exited the far door together. They turned away from her, heading toward the port's center so she couldn't see their faces. One wore navy slacks and a blue sweater. The other wore black pants, and a blue blazer topped with a captain's hat. The second man also carried a familiar tan bag. Jo thought the captain's hat would be a perfect decoy. A common technique was to give someone of the same size a distinctive bag of the same variety, then hide his features with a cap and blazer, and send him on his way.

Jo studied him for a few paces, knowing she had a call to make. Picking one person meant abandoning all others. Captain had a gait that struck her as predatory, as if he was planning to pick a fight at the bar. That convinced her he was Michael, ninety percent anyway. Perhaps the wardrobe change wasn't meant to throw off anyone behind him, but rather someone ahead. He wasn't headed back to the *Anzhelika*.

She dropped deck to deck without letting him out of her sight, like a lifeguard dismounting a tower. Then she began to run, rolling her feet to muffle the noise. Jo continued at a jog until there was just thirty meters between them and then dropped her pace. She closed to twenty-five meters and then twenty. This was closer than her handlers at Langley would advise, but she was flexing with the circumstances.

She was armed with a slimline subcompact Glock and a directional microphone. If she could see it, she could shoot it and listen to its final breath. But not from thirty meters. She was pushing both her pistol marksmanship and her microphone's capabilities at twenty.

"How's it going?" Achilles asked.

"I'm on him. He changed into a captain's hat and blazer. We're still walking."

"Interesting. He changed for a purpose, you can be sure of that. Something's up."

"I'm on it. What's going on with you?"

"I happen to be changing as well. I'm down in the crew quarters, putting on a waiter's uniform."

"What will you do if someone asks you for something?"

"Do my best to be obsequious."

"I meant that they're likely to ask you in Russian."

"I'm fluent. My mother was from Moscow. Speak of the devil, I gotta go. Be careful."

As Achilles signed off, Michael turned right and stepped onto a yacht, the *Daisy Mae*.

Jo pulled out her phone and pretended to type while

watching him.

He went up the back staircase to the level above, where a man's head and shoulders popped into view as he stood to shake Michael's hand.

She glanced at the time on her screen. Exactly 9:00. Michael had an appointment with someone. She didn't know who or why, but intuition told her that it was mission critical to find out.

Chapter 14

Interference

"WHO ARE YOU?"

"Agent Achilles, this is Director Rider, looking for a sitrep."

The two incongruous questions hit me at the same time. The first, spoken in Russian, came from a large man in a waiter's uniform identical to the one I'd just slipped on. I'd have to answer it first, which meant the head of the CIA was about to become confused while he waited for his situation report. Normally I'd switch my ear mike off to spare us both the confusion, but that movement would look peculiar, and at this moment I needed to appear anything but. "I'm Volodya's replacement, Vanya. Pleased to meet you."

The intruder's expression changed. "Which Volodya?"

"I'm not sure."

"Dubnov? Was it Dubnov?"

"I'm not sure. His last name wasn't mentioned."

"I hope not, but I wouldn't put it past Stepashin. He'll fire anyone for anything. You better hurry up. It's crazy up there, and Mister Voskerchyan doesn't like crazy." His eyes appraised me, head to toe. Seeming to approve, he said, "Take my advice and work to appear calm and deferential at all times, no matter what these spoiled bastards say or do. By the way, I'm Pavel. Gotta run."

"What the hell is going on?" Director Rider asked in my ear.

Pavel turned and began to exit but then stopped short. Two other guys walked past him into the room. Pavel turned back around. "This is Volodya Dubnov," he said, pointing to a thick man with wrestler's ears on his left. "And this is Volodya Mendelson." He pointed toward his right, to a handsome guy whose height and build were more suited for the NFL than a cruise ship. "Which one are you replacing?"

The gig was up. Pavel's expression told me he knew he'd been played, and wasn't happy about it. I was oh for two on finesse today, and the stakes were mounting with each failure. This time I was facing a veritable wall of opposition. At 6'2" and 220 pounds, I'm no powder puff, but these three were close to that on average, accent on the three.

"Mister Voskerchyan doesn't like thieves or spies," Pavel continued. "Which one are you?"

Wrestler spoke next, confirming that Pavel's

question was rhetorical. "Last guy we caught provided us with a week's worth of entertainment before we let the sharks in on the fun. It gets boring down here in the crew quarters, you see. All the good stuff is up top. So thanks for joining us, regardless of your reason."

"International waters are like outer space," Handsome added. "Nobody can hear you scream."

While they were busy working themselves up as men do before combat, I was assessing the situation. The trick was going to be rendering them unconscious without inflicting permanent damage or worse. Although the more they talked, the less I was concerned about the worse. Keep talking, guys. Given the close-quarters combat environment, I pegged Wrestler as the biggest threat and decided to take him out first.

"Let's go talk to Voskerchyan," I said, raising doubt as I moved toward them and the door.

The uppercut has several advantages, one of which is that it's delivered through the undefended territory between the arms. Another advantage to uppercuts is that they slip in below the visual field. Recipients often never see them coming. That was exactly what happened to Wrestler. "Nobody gets-" was as far as he got before my palm-heel strike turned off his lights. If there had been onlookers, they'd have said, "He never knew what hit him."

With the other two just off to my left, I spun around and put my right elbow into Pavel's solar plexus with enough force to lift him off the ground with a grunt and a whoosh. Solar plexus blows are beautiful because they cause all kinds of stress. The recipient remains conscious, but his system goes into reboot as it reacts to the systemic disruption that just paralyzed his diaphragm and stole all his air.

Continuing around with my circular momentum, I attempted to place a crushing yoke strike against Handsome's larynx. I was fast, but not fast enough, and he snapped his head back in time to dodge the brunt of it. I continued through with my planned combination, planting a powerful left cross on Pavel's temple and sending him to dreamland with a headache that would reverberate for weeks.

Dodging a kick from Handsome, I put myself between him and the door. The expression on his face told me he thought I was going to run for it, but I kicked it closed instead.

As the lock clicked home, the right side of his mouth pulled back in a primordial smile, revealing his canine tooth. Apparently Voskerchyan staffed his yacht with men who could serve a dual purpose. Being the bigger guy, and thinking I was cornered, Handsome launched himself at me as if he was storming the castle gate. His intent seemed to be to crush me where I stood, a bug on the windshield of his brawn.

I shot my left hand forward as though I was going for his eyes. Nothing induces panic faster than an ocular assault. As he tilted and twisted his head, I hit the other panic button. I drove my right fist straight into his balls, fast and true. Momentum carried him into me and flattened me against the door, but he doubled over rather than pushing through. A quick rabbit punch knocked him out.

"I repeat. What the hell is going on?" The voice in my ear was still talking. "You're not in direct contact, are you Achilles?"

Direct contact was a literal description of what I was doing, but Rider didn't need to know that. "Hold on, sir."

I got busy stuffing three oversized sailors into three undersized wardrobes. The result wasn't pretty, but I got all the doors closed and locked with keys from their pockets.

Time to deal with Rider, one way or another. I considered switching off the mike now that I was alone, but it was about to get hairy, and I knew I might need support. "Sir, I'm aboard the yacht where we believe Ivan is meeting Emily."

"What do you mean you believe?"

Their syntax was so similar that I wondered if Rider was secretly Oscar's father. "Emily was brought here, we believe, as part of Ivan's plan to influence the London mayoral election, but I don't have visual confirmation. The Anzhelika is the size of a football field, so I've changed into a crew uniform to facilitate the search. I need to get on that now, sir."

"You do that. Don't plan to disembark while Ivan's still breathing."

Chapter 15

Show and Tell

"I'VE BROUGHT SOMETHING with me. A little show and tell that I guarantee will change your life." Speaking to the mayoral candidate, Michael's tone made it clear that his words should not be construed as hyperbole.

Lounging before a gas-and-glass fire pit at the aft end of the *Daisy Mae's* big deck, Kian Aspinwall appeared as relaxed as a politician in the midst of a high-profile campaign can be. He wore a pink button-down beneath a blue linen blazer, and boat shoes on bare feet. Keeping his eyes on Michael's, and flashing a pleasant smile that showed plenty of perfect teeth, he replied, "I'm intrigued."

So was Jo.

She'd crept to a perch on a neighboring yacht that gave her line of sight on the conversing couple. From that vantage point, her directional microphone delivered their words as clearly as if she'd been seated with them.

She was reveling in her good luck when Michael lifted his tan leather bag and said, "Let's move to the table."

Her heart sank, her lips mouthing, "Merde."

That ruined everything.

When they moved back toward the main saloon, she'd lose sight and sound. Even worse, there was no location on her yacht that gave a downward angle on that table. To see what was in the bag, she was literally going to have to jump ship — silently, invisibly, and immediately.

Jo jammed her equipment back into her purse. As she slipped off her boots and socks, the internal monologue began. *What are you doing, Jo? My job. Don't think about the risks, just do it.*

She backed up to the far railing, took a deep breath, and then started sprinting. Five strides to gain speed, then up onto a footstool with her left, then the guardrail with her right, followed by an open-air dive — arms forward, legs up, eyes locked on the guardrail of the *Daisy Mae's* top deck some ten feet away.

If she missed, she'd likely drop three stories to the water. Noise. Injury. Attention. Failure. She let the consequences fly by as fast as the scenery, maintaining her focus on victory.

The instant her fingers touched precious chrome, Jo used core strength and momentum to pike her hips up, flipping her legs over like she'd done a thousand times on the uneven bars. She released her grip on the rail as soon as her ankles broke the vertical plane, and a split second later landed — on her ass. Her pride took a hit, but she was none the worse for wear.

After scrambling to her feet, Jo pulled the monocular and directional mike from her bag, and scurried to the far edge. Peering over, she found the corner of the wall separating the saloon from the aft deck. She wriggled under the guardrail on her belly at that spot, and then slid over the edge.

Hanging with her knees crooked over the middle beam of the guardrail above, she maneuvered to an angle that let her see the table over Kian Aspinwall's shoulder. Covert surveillance Batman-style had never come to mind while practicing inversions in yoga class, but it likely would hereafter.

As she redirected the mike, she heard Aspinwall say, "After your introduction, I wasn't expecting fruit."

"Ah, but when is citrus not fruit?" Michael replied.

Jo saw that he'd placed a grapefruit on the table, atop a little trivet that held it steady.

Kian's expression hinted at the perplexed indifference that Jo suspected he was feeling. Perplexed, because this was no doubt the most unusual one-on-one meeting he'd hosted all day. Indifferent, because the thousands of pounds Michael had no doubt contributed to his campaign for the privilege were already in the bank.

Michael then withdrew a manila envelope from his

bag.

The thought of blackmail photos crossed Jo's mind before he slid an unfamiliar object out and it clunked onto the table. It was a loop of wire joined by a metal puck the size of a large coin, but about four times as thick.

"That's interesting," Kian said, his confusion obviously mounting.

"Isn't it," Michael replied.

He proceeded to belt the grapefruit with the wire, securing it at the equator by pulling the ends tight. "Now comes the cool part."

Chapter 16

Range-R

"DON'T PLAN TO DISEMBARK while Ivan's still breathing." I repeated Rider's words to myself as I fastened my black tie. The man had sounded like a saint during his Senate confirmation hearing. All polite and prim and proper. Politicians were a different species. But I was happy enough with the plan.

I'd boarded the *Anzhelika* under the guise of being an advance member of Prince Albert's security detail. This had resonated with the matched set of Russian thugs at the bottom of the gangplank, as it made me a brother-in-arms of sorts.

That didn't stop them from confiscating my Glock.

Losing my firearm was a setback, but not critical. I could kill Ivan with anything from a shoelace to a copy of Vanity Fair, although I'd prefer the speed of something more conventional.

I made my way down the hall toward the galley in search of camouflaging props and more conventional weapons.

The galley was a veritable beehive. White-hatted chefs were checking and chopping, while the arms of assistants flew about their production stations. Chicly attired servers came and went, deftly carting away culinary masterpieces on silver platters.

My stomach began to growl like a belligerent dog at the smell of bacon-wrapped scallops. I was overdue for dinner. An approaching waitress heard the rumble and gave me a look.

"Where can I get a bottle of Cristal Champagne?"

She began to answer without breaking her stride, but then caught my eye and paused. "You're new. But then you wouldn't be asking the question if you weren't, I suppose. I'm Tanya."

"Vayna. Pleased to meet you."

Tanya was a dark-haired beauty whose long legs made the most of her stylish uniform. She gave me a smile so warm I worried it would bake the rare Ahi tuna on her plate. "The wine store is one level down toward the bow, with the other cold storage. Alex will help you."

I said, "Thanks," and grabbed a couple of her hors d'oeuvres with my right hand while my left surreptitiously slipped the long silver corkscrew from her apron.

She winked and was gone.

I inspected my new weapon on the way to cold

storage, while making the Ahi vanish. It was a three-for-one deal. The foil knife was small but very sharp. Probably Swiss. Well-tailored for windpipes and carotids. The actual corkscrew swung out of the middle to form a T. Protruding between my middle and ring fingers, it would work as a knuckle-duster, debilitating major muscles, and wreaking havoc on throats and eyes. Finally, the blunt end would function like a Kubotan stick. Lethal on the temples, and good for debilitating blows to bony areas and sensitive fleshy spots. Best of all, it looked innocuous.

I found Alex as advertised. He was mid-sixties if not older — the oldest guy I'd seen working. Also the most relaxed. I guessed he'd been with Voskerchyan since before the Berlin Wall came down. "A bottle of Cristal?" I asked, by way of greeting.

"Semechkin must have arrived," he said, his voice unexpectedly low. "Coming right up."

I had no idea who Semechkin was, but when luck smiles you smile back. I accepted the bottle in an iced silver bucket along with two crystal flutes and the obligatory silver platter.

Oscar had sent the *Anzhelika's* deck plan to my smartphone. What a monster. But as big as she was, I only spotted a few likely haunts for Ivan and Emily. Those included the saloons, the open decks, and the guest rooms. Since the common areas were crawling with both hostile eyes and thirsty guests, I decided to try the cabins first.

They were two levels up.

As I headed for the stairs, I wondered how Jo was faring. Her moves picking the pockets of the prince's entourage had impressed me, as much for the strategic thinking it represented as for her tactical execution. She must have had quite a time at The Farm, using her quick wits to compensate for a lack of prior training.

I could relate to that.

I looked forward to learning more about her story over a beer, once we'd taken Ivan out.

I paused on the stairwell to study the main saloon through the open lobby doors. It looked like the red carpet at the Academy Awards. There were enough jewels on display to pay off Greece's national debt, and a wide enough range of beauty to supply an entire Miss Universe pageant. I would have enjoyed mingling for an hour or two, just to pick up tips on which islands to buy, and where to acquire the most obedient slaves, but I limited my exposure to a quick scan of faces.

Emily's wasn't among them.

Worried that I'd be flagged down like the lone waiter in an overcrowded diner, I completed my ascent when most heads were turned, and ducked into the hallway that led back to the guest rooms. Despite the *Anzhelika's* size, there were only seven. A literal interpretation of living large.

I'd formulated my plan of attack while Alex was

placing the Cristal in the bucket. Noting the shape and recalling the weight of the last bottle I'd hefted, I realized he was handing me a club. It would only be good for a surprise blow or two, but surprise was exactly what I intended.

Posing as a daft and misdirected waiter, I'd key into promising rooms until I found Ivan. At that point, there would be a bit of quarrelsome dialogue including *who ordered what* and *now that I'm here*, followed a few days later by a headline reading: *The Champagne went to his head.*

I whipped out the Range-R and began walking down the left side of the corridor, pressing it against the wall with my left hand while my right supported the Champagne.

The Range-R Xtreme was like a sophisticated stud finder that painted a picture of bodies in a room. Very cool. Of the seven staterooms, only two contained animate objects. The third on the left had a couple I was quite certain were naked, and the VIP suite at the end contained a trio I was equally certain were not. Neither room looked particularly promising, but tactically there was a smart place to start. I wasn't worried about dying from embarrassment.

Chapter 17

Pushing Buttons

JO MENTALLY URGED Michael to hurry as he set his cell phone down on the table, and opened an app. Her calves were really wailing now.

She was dangling face down over the rail, hooked by the crook in her legs. She'd been crossing and uncrossing her ankles to shift the weight, but that no longer helped. Soon they would give out and she'd drop. At least her plan was working. By using the monocular's fine-tuning, she'd brought the phone's screen into sharp focus.

As Kian watched, oblivious to Michael's sinister intentions, the app came to life. It displayed red, yellow, and green buttons on the left, and a slider switch on the right. "The slider controls the wire's length," Michael said, his tone making this achievement out to be the equivalent of cold fusion. To demonstrate, he slid it until the grapefruit looked like a fat man in a tight belt.

Michael shifted his gaze to Kian, obviously

expecting a reaction.

"Fascinating. What do the buttons do?"

"Green is the release," Michael said, extending his index finger with a flourish. He ceremoniously tapped the screen, causing the wire to slacken and the puck to thunk onto the table. "It's heavier than it looks. Now, I want you to remember that button. It's going to be very important later on.

"Next is yellow. When I tap yellow, like so, the belt begins to tighten. The Swiss precision is too slow to see, but trust me, it's moving." He lifted the widget by the puck, and sure enough, after about ten seconds it was tight enough that he could remove his hand without it falling.

"Now, as you might guess, red is the opposite of green. Would you care for the honor?" He proffered the phone, as the grapefruit began to pucker.

Ever the gentleman, Aspinwall mimicked Michael's fanfare as he pressed the red button.

The wire cinched like a hangman's noose, and the grapefruit burst open, sending sticky pink juice spraying in all directions. A second later, the puck clattered to the table and Michael lifted the top half of the grapefruit clean off. "No breakfast table should be without one."

Jo thought Aspinwall was doing a great job of maintaining an enthusiastic face, despite being confronted with what appeared to be a late-night infomercial reject, at the end of a long campaign day.

Again his response was politely ambiguous. "I've never seen anything like it."

Michael held up a finger, asking Aspinwall to hold that thought. Then he swapped apps on his phone. Again he propped it up on the table so they both could see the screen. Jo strained to get the right new visual angle, adding a cramping back to her list of discomforts. Just a few seconds more, she repeated for the dozenth time.

While both Kian and Jo watched with rapt attention, Michael tapped the screen and the image of a woman appeared. Jo didn't recognize the face — she'd never been close enough for that — but she did recognize the dress. It was Emily Aspinwall.

"What is this?" Aspinwall asked, his tone no longer entirely cordial. "Why are you showing me a video of my daughter?"

Jo studied the picture. The first thing that struck her was that the image was being captured by a lapel camera. The centering was off, as was the angle, and the focus was less than perfect. It was just like the footage shot during her undercover training assignments.

The second thing that struck her was the location. Based on the background, she knew where Emily was standing. She needed to let Achilles know, but this wasn't the time to break away.

"It's showtime, Ivan," Michael said.

Aspinwall looked around for the recipient of Michael's remark, but didn't see anybody.

Michael redirected his host's attention to the screen.

A hand had popped up in front of the lapel camera. It was holding a smartphone open to the same red-yellow-green button app they'd just seen demonstrated. The hand held it there for a good ten seconds, then the hand dropped and the cameraman moved. He turned Emily toward the railing so that they were both looking out over the Mediterranean, where dozens of festive yachts lit up the harbor.

Jo could almost hear music crescendo as the hand on the camera moved to Emily's shoulder like Jaws coming out of the deep. As the fingers clamped around her flesh, the thumb beckoned for attention. It was tapping against the clasp of her necklace — a clasp that was decorated like a moon, but shaped like a puck.

Chapter 18

Revelations

"I HAVE A CONFESSION to make," Emily said, staring out at the panorama of bobbing yachts and twinkling stars.

"You can tell me anything, except goodbye," Andreas said, his hand caressing the back of her neck.

She turned to face him. A string of white bow lights reflected in his eyes like a stairway to heaven. "I've never been as happy as I am now, at this very moment. I thought men like you existed only in dreams."

Andreas replied so softly, she had to strain to hear him over the wind and slapping waves. "You bring out the best in me."

"I'm sorry. I suppose that sounded sappy. I'm not usually like that. It's just that online, you seemed too good to be true. But I held onto hope, and now I have proof that you're real."

"I understand."

"Do you? Yes, of course you do. That's kind of my

point. I was just, well, so ready for tonight to be a disappointment. Back in London, I mean. And then with all of this," she gestured with both arms. "It's … people always hide the bad things online. You only hid good things, starting with your handsome face. Usually it's the ugly guys who post blurry pictures. And your lifestyle. Not even a coded hint. I just didn't know guys like you really existed. And there I go again."

Andreas said, "Let's forget about the past, and stop worrying about the future, and just enjoy the moment."

She stood quietly, contentedly, studying his face.

It gave her a different kind of surprise.

He'd had work done.

Not Botox or hair transplants, but reconstructive work. It was expertly done, but she knew from a summer internship in her uncle's office how to spot the scars. And his eyes, they weren't naturally blue. He was wearing colored lenses. All this was normal for the superyacht crowd, she felt sure, but it struck her as out of character for Andreas. He was like her, more Labrador than poodle. "How do you know our host?"

"Voskerchyan? I do work for him from time to time. Perks like this are part of our retainer arrangement."

If this is a perk, Emily thought, *the base pay must be fantastic*. "You never told me exactly what kind of consulting it is you do."

Fireworks erupted with a boom and a series of smaller pops. The first salvo of the evening. Andreas had told her there would be a display to mark the end of the show. Since the best viewing was aft, he'd invited her to the bow, where they could enjoy some privacy. She appreciated the romantic gesture. She was also pleased when Andreas ignored the display in order to give her an answer.

Speaking loudly to be heard over the booms, oohs, and aahs, he said, "My work doesn't really fit in a box. I'm trustworthy, and good at solving problems. Men like Voskerchyan need people they can trust, and they tend to have lots of-"

Still looking at the decorative lights reflecting in Andreas's eyes, Emily saw them cloud over as his words suddenly ground to a halt. His face followed with an almost schizophrenic transformation, shifting from warm honey to iced steel. Her elation turned to that heart-stopping fear one gets when the doctor looks up from the x-ray and says, "Bad news."

Chapter 19

Leashed

JO FOUND herself completely entranced by the scene unfolding before her eyes. Her screaming calves and groaning shoulders had faded to background noise, so engrossing was the human drama unraveling on the deck below.

A minute earlier, when Michael had closed the app to heighten Kian's tension, she'd ripped away to alert Achilles of her findings. She had filled him in on Emily and Ivan's location, along with the devious device The Ghost had surreptitiously strung around her neck.

When she bobbed back down to watch the saga play out, Aspinwall appeared to have no blood going to his face. She appreciated his condition.

A single synaptic connection, a literal flash of understanding, had sent him from the top of the world to the bottom of a boot. He was reeling from the change of altitude. He was lost. The righteous indignation and false bravado that were often the bedrock of a politician's defenses had no place in discussions involving the safety of their children.

Michael was waiting patiently for Aspinwall to come to the conclusion that he was in checkmate. His only move was the one prescribed. Whatever it might be.

When he finally spoke, Aspinwall's voice was little more than a whisper. "What do I have to do?"

Michael's reply was forceful and quick. "Bring me the head of Prince Albert."

"What!"

Michael held his gaze, unflinching. He let Aspinwall's imagination run amok with medieval images of swords and sacks and silver platters, dead eyes and distended tongues and bloodied blades. "Just kidding, Kian. All you need to do is go to His Highness's reception, as planned, and make a simple statement to the press."

"I don't have to hurt anybody?"

Michael shook his head.

"And Emily will be okay?"

"If you're fast enough, she'll never even know she came within a finger tap of a slow and agonizing death. She'll never even imagine the feel of steel closing around her throat, or the overwhelming terror that seizes the mind when lungs are powerless to inflate. She'll finish off her date completely oblivious to the fact that she spent this evening dancing on the brink, and will go home having enjoyed the best day of her life. If you're fast enough."

"What do I have to say?"

"Does it matter?"

Aspinwall paused.

"You're wasting time, Kian."

"No, it doesn't matter."

Michael handed him a slip of paper that Jo couldn't see. "Read this out loud. For practice."

Jo watched Aspinwall's face run a gamut of emotions before she heard the words, "It's so nice here, I'm dreading going back to London."

It took her a second to appreciate the brilliance of the simple sentence.

It was a smart bomb.

The statement was so plausible, both for its context and its content, that nobody would expect coercion. Who hadn't made a similar statement while on vacation to someplace as magical as this? But the media would be on Aspinwall's words like tigers on red meat. Their spin would be relentless. Pundits would come out of the woodwork, disillusioned supporters would be interviewed, outrage would be voiced, all feeding the machine that never slept. Aspinwall hadn't just implied that the city many considered the finest in the world, the city he was vying to lead, was "not so nice." He made it clear that he preferred his nation's historical rival.

It was suicide by Freudian slip.

"Your delivery was a bit flat," Michael said. "But

I'm sure you'll perk up in front of the cameras, with the prince in the room and the Monaco Yacht Show logo over your shoulder."

Aspinwall swallowed a frog as he nodded. "What kind of guarantee do I have?"

Michael shook his head in disappointment. "The common sense kind, Kian. We could have kidnapped Emily and dangled her over a kennel of starving dogs. But that's not our style. We'd only do that if you attempted a retraction.

"Instead, we've gone to extravagant lengths to come and go like a bad dream. Tomorrow, there will be no trace of our existence but the footprints on your mind. In time, even you'll begin to doubt that this was real."

"When will the necklace come off?"

"The moment you step off the media stage, assuming we approve of your performance, of course. You'll be able to watch it happen. I'll open the app back up and hold the phone where you can see it the whole time you're speaking, lest your political instincts kick in and your feet get cold. If that happens, you'll be watching Emily's head come off rather than the necklace."

Michael stood and headed for the stairs.

Aspinwall followed like a leashed dog.

Chapter 20

Yellow

WHILE A LUMP FORMED in her throat, Emily studied her date's facial transformation in the colorful cascade of firework light. When Andreas resumed speaking, it wasn't to her, and his voice had dropped an octave. "You were at Palace Place this morning. I saw you on Michael's button cam." As he spoke, Andreas raised his cell phone, but not to his ear. He was holding it up like a police officer's badge. The phone showed something resembling a traffic light, with buttons of red, yellow, and green.

Emily glanced at the phone, and then at the man Andreas had directed it toward. The waiter had indeed been in her lobby this morning, wearing a gray suit. He'd helped her with the door. Justine's new boyfriend, she'd assumed.

The back of her neck began to tickle.

She reached for her necklace, afraid that it was slipping off. The pendant wasn't there. She began to panic but then found it, higher up rather than lower. She'd adjust it later, as soon as this odd twist was resolved, and her fairy tale had resumed. "You *were* there," she said, addressing the man. "Who are you? Are you following me?"

He responded to her, but didn't take his eyes off Andreas. "I work in law enforcement. I'm here to rescue you." Then his voice took on a commanding tone. "Step away from her, Ivan."

Emily appraised the man while he spoke. The set of his jaw and the energy radiating from his eyes told her he was deadly serious. His body looked serious too, primed and physically fit. Andreas was in good shape as well, but his fitness struck her as the health club type. *More show than go*, as Jen liked to say. Plus, Andreas was smaller by about two inches and twenty pounds. "You're mistaken," she said, pressing herself against Andreas and wrapping her arm around his waist. "I don't need rescuing, and his name isn't Ivan, it's Andreas. Please leave us alone."

His expression softened and he shifted his gaze to meet her eye. For a second she thought he was going to say, "My mistake. I'm obviously confused. Please forgive me." Instead he put ice in her spine. "Everything you know about him is a lie, Emily. He spied on you to learn what you like, and then told you what you wanted to hear. All this is about manipulating your father into dropping out of the race."

"How do you know that?" Andreas asked.

The question caused Emily to do a double take. It wasn't a denial or even a challenge. Andreas sounded as if he sincerely wanted to know.

She turned to study him.

Andreas's eyes were locked on the stranger's. His expression, in fact his whole face, had morphed. His look was now positively carnivorous. He continued to hold up his cell phone as if it was a mystical amulet with protective powers.

"Does it matter?" the intruder asked.

"At the moment, the only thing that matters is what I can do with this." Andreas waved his phone. "Do you know? I'm talking about the yellow button in particular."

"I know," the intruder said.

Emily had no idea what the yellow button would do, but she was quite certain that she didn't want to find out. She didn't understand Andreas's next words either, but something about the way he said them made her shiver.

"Well then, you've got a choice to make."

He paused, his face brandishing an evil expression she'd never forget. Then he pressed the yellow button.

Chapter 21

Press Conference

JO WAITED for Michael and Kian to disappear down the stairs and then swung down to the deck they'd abandoned. She managed to execute the swing itself as planned, but her cramped legs refused to take her weight when she landed. She ended up dancing with a deck chair that first whacked her funny bone and then bloodied her nose.

Sitting up where she eventually landed, Jo stretched her legs by grabbing her feet and bringing her face to her knees. Then she gave her calves a couple of quick squeezes while wiping her nose on her pants.

Michael and Aspinwall were disappearing down the dock to her right as she used the railing to pull herself to her feet, but her legs were still tingling. Pushing through the pain, she did a few calf raises to get the blood flowing, and then set off barefoot in pursuit.

The dock was busy as a holiday mall once again. The sun had set on Saturday night, which made Monaco the place to be if one owned an impressive yacht and had millions to spend. The female revelers had swapped their shorts and sandals for pumps and gowns, lavish silky creations designed to parade augmented breasts and display ostentatious jewels. As for the men, they seemed to be evenly split, with half taking their fashion advice from the Robb Report, and the rest mimicking James Bond.

Anxious to learn of Achilles' progress and update him on Michael's plan, Jo tried to key her ear mike and found that it wasn't there. *Merde!* It must have popped out when she fell.

Her stomach seemed to shrink as the ramifications set in. In an instant she'd gone from the comfort of a protective wing, to feeling totally alone. A bird pushed out of the nest and onto the ground.

Jo tried to shake the solitary feeling as she took up Michael's tail. In her head she knew it was silly. She'd been alone her whole adult life, whereas she'd only known Achilles for a couple of hours. He wasn't even there anyway, not physically. *This didn't change a thing*, she told herself. He had his mission, and now she had hers.

Or did she?

As long as Ivan was still alive, she was going to stick with Michael — whatever it took. But what should she do once Ivan was dead? Director Rider had been crystal clear about his one and only goal: kill Ivan without getting caught. If Achilles hadn't accomplished that already, he soon would. And Michael would see it happen.

What would she do then?

Achilles had repeatedly warned her not to engage Michael, but could she just let him get away? She'd have to play that by ear. Meanwhile, she was dying to see what would happen on camera.

Michael guided Aspinwall to the Upper Deck Lounge, which sat atop the marina offices. The MYS organizers had the large room arranged like the red carpet at a movie premiere. A cocktail lounge by day, it was now a hub for the press to interview the yacht manufacturers, billionaire owners, and scores of major and minor celebrities in attendance.

The network stations were packing up after the prince's concluding remarks, but plenty of local and tabloid reporters had stuck around in hopes of recording gaffs and revelations once the vodka and Cognac started flowing.

Michael appeared to have a particular reporter in mind, as he led Aspinwall straight to a petite blonde on dangerously high heels. She was probably north of forty but would pass for twenty-nine on camera thanks to heavy makeup, a starvation diet, and hair extensions. Jo didn't recognize the flag on her microphone, but assumed she was British.

Michael showed Aspinwall the script one last time,

and then stood back so the candidate could make a solo approach. While Michael's eyes were locked on his target, Jo sidled up to hers.

Aspinwall turned to face the crowd, with the wall of Monaco Yacht Show logos behind him, and the selected reporter eagerly waiting in front.

Jo had to hand it to him. The man was a master of his own emotions. He was about to commit suicide on camera, but he seemed lively, even enthusiastic. No doubt he was flying on autopilot using the same campaign-trail reflexes that kept him engaging while repeating a stump speech night after night.

Michael stood directly beside the petite reporter. As she tested her mike, he relaunched the app and extended his smartphone toward the honored guest as though he was recording a video, rather than playing one. It was a smooth setup, and one he'd obviously planned. Only Aspinwall could see the display.

With the reverberation of the evening's first fireworks providing a fitting backdrop, the reporter began recording. "I'm Sandra Sunnyford, here now with Kian Aspinwall, MP from Croydon, and leading candidate in the London mayoral election. Tell us, Mister Aspinwall, did you enjoy the show?"

Chapter 22

Overboard

UNLIKE MOST of my colleagues in the CIA's Special Operation's Group, I was not a combat veteran. I'd been climbing cliffs and chasing Olympic gold while they were earning green berets and golden tridents. But just because I wasn't used to people shooting at me, didn't mean I hadn't developed combat reflexes.

There's something about hanging 200 meters up by the last knuckle on the left index finger that stimulates growth in the quick-response part of the brain. So by the time Ivan had released the yellow button, I had launched into action.

Before she had gone incommunicado, Jo had briefly described the remote controlled garrote with its slider and three buttons. Armed with that information, I'd formulated my plan of attack the moment Ivan had raised the phone. Forewarned is forearmed, as they say.

Having abandoned the ice bucket and glasses in favor of just carrying the Cristal club, I flung it like a lawn dart straight at Ivan's head. Given the twenty feet between us, I wasn't expecting a hit but rather a distraction while I covered the gap. Launching myself at his phone with the force and focus of a guided missile, I was absolutely determined that nothing would stop me until I hit green. No man, no machine, no weapon, no wound.

My preprogramming didn't stop with a quick sprint and phone grab. The instant my right arm found the green button and put Emily beyond threat, I'd be redirecting my momentum into whipping around. I'd channel it down my right arm and shoulder, then into my back, where it would be joined by the power my thighs were kicking in. By the time my left elbow transferred all my kinetic energy into Ivan's head, it would be packing the power of Barry Bond's bat. I'd smash the side of his skull with such force that his spinal cord would sever and his brain would splatter like a melon catapulted against a castle wall. Four seconds from game on to game over.

All accompanied by a delightful fireworks display.

At least that was how I had it choreographed out in my head.

The Ghost had another plan.

He surprised me. Not once, or twice, but three times, beginning with the *you've got a choice to make* taunt that initiated my blitzkrieg attack. Then he surprised me a second time by slipping the Cristal attack with a calm dip of his head and tilt of his shoulder. The Ghost was cool under fire, no doubt about that. But the most startling surprise was his game-changing third.

Ivan had no warning that he'd picked up a tail. As Director Rider had repeatedly reminded me, this was the first time in eight years it had happened. In that context, I'd focused my mental energies on trying to understand the anomaly that led to the exception, rather than the personality that created the rule. I overlooked the implications inherent in dealing with a man who had avoided not just capture, but even detection, for many years.

I had been so wrapped up in the notion of catching Ivan unaware, that I forgot to account for the fact that regardless of the circumstance or situation, a man like The Ghost would *always always always* have an escape plan.

Ivan didn't have to scheme when I miraculously appeared. He just had to activate the contingency that was already in his head.

By the time my sprinting feet were halfway to their mark, he'd sent the phone spinning up and off to the left like a clay skeet fired from the bow. And while my processor was busy dealing with that targeting dilemma, Ivan threw another curveball, by vaulting over the rail to the right.

I didn't go left or right.

I made the choice Ivan predicted.

The woman I'd watched being lured from her home, the woman who had unknowingly placed her life in my hands, was now just seconds from a horrible death in the middle.

"Forget the girl, go after Ivan!" Director Rider's voice boomed like an explosion inside my head.

He must have had me on satellite.

I ignored him.

As Emily dropped to her knees, her hands at her neck and her teary eyes wide with panic, I adapted my plan. I didn't try to reassure her, or coach her, or explain. I just went for her throat.

My fingers aren't dainty tools, and my hands aren't designed to be tender. I'm your guy if you need walnuts cracked, or large jars opened, or a steaming moose extricated from the grill of your car. But I was determined to make do with what the good Lord gave me.

I attacked the necklace from behind, where the chain fed through the clasp. After digging my index fingers underneath the chain as if they were ice-cream scoops, I placed one on either side of the platinum moon and pinched down hard on the chain with my thumbs. I could feel the ratcheting action working, the precision of a Swiss watch paired with the power of a bell tower clock.

It didn't stop.

"Forget about her, Agent Achilles!" the Director

boomed again. "That's a direct order. Ivan is priority one."

I wedged my thumbnails in right where the cable disappeared into the clasp, and then matched the move with my index fingers. While Emily gasped, I squeezed.

The mechanism faltered, its gears unable to turn.

I'd halted the progression, but that wasn't good enough. I could feel Emily falling into unconsciousness, her brain reeling from a lack of blood. I yelled, "Hold on!" to her, to Rider, and to myself.

Anyone who has ever used a zip-tie knows the power of a ratchet. The little plastic tail feeds easily through the mouth in one direction, but it's virtually impossible to force the reverse. The physics are so effective that law enforcement often uses zip-ties instead of handcuffs.

A Special Forces master sergeant named Dix had taught me the secret to defeating them. By delivering an explosive burst of energy — a violent lightning thrust against an immobile object combined with a wrenching hand twist — the ratchet could be overpowered. Of course this tactic also wreaks havoc on the wrists, but for captured undercover operatives a superficial flesh wound was considerably better than the likely alternative. In Emily's case, however, an explosive burst was not an option. Throats were far more tender, and infinitely less forgiving, than wrists.

So what was I to do? I had no leverage.

I had the corkscrew's foil blade in my pocket, but to reach it I'd have to release the chain. While I worked to get the blade wedged into place, the gears would grind on. Even if I got it under before she died, cutting the chain wasn't going to be like severing string. While plated in platinum, the core cable was obviously made of high tensile strength steel. My knife might never cut it.

I did the only thing I could do.

I went for broke.

Emily was about to expire in my arms, so we had nothing to lose. "Hold on!" I yelled again, digging my middle fingers in beside my indexes. The additional tension drew blood from Emily's throat, but it also changed the physics. Instead of pincers pressing a single point of contact, my thumbs were now like pliers braced against two pads. I squeezed them with everything I had, and then I squeezed more. I pictured them digging in, biting down, clamping on. No longer were my fingers instruments of flesh and bone. They were the hardened steel jaws of a metalworker's vise.

Then I engaged the hydraulic press.

My forearms clenched, my biceps bunched, and my shoulders began to pull. Like oxen trying to wrench a stump from the ground, they tensed and tightened and pulled and strained until all at once something popped, and the clasp released.

Emily was free.

I lay her down and checked her throat. Blood was streaming where the rays of the golden sun had dug in, but it wasn't spurting. Her carotids weren't sliced, but her windpipe was sucking air. I pressed my left thumb over the tiny hole, and slapped her face with the palm of my right hand. "Emily! Emily, wake up! Wake up!"

Her eyes sprang open and she began to cough, drawing deep ragged breaths, as she reflexively tried to push my hand from her throat.

"Don't do that. You've got a small puncture in your windpipe. It's not life-threatening, but you should keep the pressure on." I guided her right hand into position. "Go straight to a hospital. They'll fix you right up."

"You've done all you can for her," Rider boomed. "Get going after Ivan."

This time, I agreed.

How long had it been? How much of a lead did he have? Was it closer to five seconds or five minutes? It felt like an eternity, and for Emily it nearly had been, but I knew that adrenaline did funny things with time.

"You're going to be all right," I said. Then I followed Ivan over the rail.

Chapter 23

Jammed

BUTTERFLIES BEGAN TO DANCE in Jo's stomach as Aspinwall's face lost all composure. It looked as if a mask had been ripped from his face, and it happened right as he was about to speak. He just stood there staring toward Michael's phone, his face awash in emotion, his gaze transfixed, the camera rolling.

Sandra, sensing a train wreck, remained silent and kept filming.

After a few seconds, Michael appeared to understand that this wasn't just the jitters. He pulled the phone back, glanced at the screen, and froze.

Jo couldn't see the screen, but she knew it had to be Achilles. Had he hit Ivan with a hollow-point round? Without sound, Ivan's head would appear to spontaneously explode. The sight of a talking head suddenly erupting from within, spewing forth blood and bone and gray matter, would give pause to even the most battle-hardened soul. Was her partner pressing the green button at that very moment, and setting Emily free?

Aspinwall said, "Forgive me, I need a minute." Then he stepped toward Michael with menace in his eyes.

Michael turned and ran for the exit.

Aspinwall followed, as did Sandra, her cameraman, and Jo.

A second after Michael turned the corner, bells began to ring and lights began to flash. He'd pulled the fire alarm.

Rounding the corner at Aspinwall's side, Jo heard the emergency exit door smacking closed a few feet ahead. The lock released as Aspinwall hit the crash-bar a second later, but the door barely moved.

Michael had blocked it with a wedge.

The fire alarm, the door jam, Jo recognized both as premeditated moves. Michael had activated a prearranged escape plan.

As Aspinwall threw himself against the bar a second time, she saw tears streaming down his cheeks, tears she recognized as anguish, not relief.

For the first time, Jo considered the possibility that something had gone wrong, that Achilles had failed and Emily was dead. Joining Aspinwall in his third attempt at the door, she asked, "Is Emily all right?"

He turned to look at her while they pressed, shock joining the anguish that ruled his face. "I don't know. The last time I saw the screen, a man was trying to save her."

The doorjamb stuttered and then gave all at once. After bursting through, Jo snatched up the black rubber wedge. She bolted down the stairs after Kian, and much faster than the encumbered cameraman or Sandra with her high heels.

Kian crashed through the door at the stairwell's bottom.

Jo joined in a split second later and recycled the wedge. Aspinwall was having a tough enough time without having his anguish caught on film.

The dock was filling up fast with people evacuating the building. Had Michael gone left, or right? Jo couldn't see him. But she knew. When the cameraman began banging on the door behind them, Jo pointed off to her left. "There he is!"

As Aspinwall ran in the wrong direction, Jo turned right. She felt bad, deceiving a man in his darkest hour of need. But the SOG's first rule was not to be seen.

Jo began to run like she'd never run before. Michael had a ten-second head start and a longer stride. She pumped her arms and pummeled her bare feet as she flew past empty exhibition tents and crowded yachts, her head down and her purse trailing. She garnered a few curses and bumped a few elbows but was making good time — until a little girl dropped her doll.

Jo was midway up the winding concrete stairs to the VIP parking lot when it happened. The girl moved into

Jo's path to retrieve her Barbie. Jo leapt up and over with momentum at her back, clearing the child but landing badly. Jamming her big toe hard enough to break it, she crashed onto the stairs before the surprised girl and her startled mother.

Chapter 24

Breathless

I FELT TERRIBLE leaving Emily in her traumatized condition. But I knew she'd be fine. She was a twenty-second walk from two-dozen spoiled mothers. She'd be on her way to the ER in under a minute. A minute on the other hand, was plenty of time for Ivan to disappear.

I hadn't seen where Ivan had landed, but I had seen exactly where he'd jumped, and I had seen precisely how. Mimicking his move from the same position, I vaulted after him.

Going over the front rail of a yacht, one would normally expect to land in the water. I had no such expectation. When Ivan had jumped, I hadn't heard a splash.

Doing exactly as he had done, I let my vaulting arm trace the rail-post as I dropped until I caught the rim of the deck, momentarily arresting my fall. I was well-practiced in this type of move from climbing rocks, but the fact that Ivan shared this skill was a clue I tucked away for future use.

Normally, arresting a vertical drop with a clamping move would have sent my legs crashing into the climbing surface, like the free end of a pendulum. But my legs met only air and kept on swinging. Expecting this after the lack of auditory feedback, I released the moment that momentum sent my center of gravity past the vertical plane. A split second later, I was standing on the next deck down.

While I was far from a superyacht aficionado, earlier in the evening I had done my share of gawking. Among the most striking features of these enormous yachts, were the luxury speedboats garaged in their hulls. Those boats, or tenders, as they're known, are hoisted in and out of the water through large garage doors. It was through one of those openings that I'd just swooped in pursuit of Ivan.

"We lost you," Director Rider said. "Agent Achilles, report."

"In pursuit. Let me focus."

I had expected to find Ivan launching a tender, but neither of the *Anzhelika's* two fine crafts were in motion. With the corkscrew readied as my weapon, I ran up the mobile staircase used for boarding and scanned the interior of both boats. Empty! I had lost Ivan.

I looked around and saw three exits.

Like game show curtains, I could only choose one.

I could go aft. I could go up. Or I could go down.

My odds of randomly picking the one Ivan had selected were just one in three. Bad enough, but illusory. The real odds were much worse. My odds would halve and halve again with every turn thereafter.

I paused to think. It wouldn't do to pick a path. I had to pick a destination.

I thought back to everything I knew about Ivan, and blended it with everything I knew about the yacht. Ivan the Ghost was a grand master at evasive tactics, and arguably better than anyone else in the world at operations planning. He was meticulous. He was audacious. And he was hell-bent on remaining invisible. How would a man like that plan to escape the *Anzhelika* if the shit hit the fan?

The general answer was trademark Ivan. Ghosts vanish. That was a start, but I had to get more specific.

How would I vanish on a superyacht?

I supposed I might just hide and hope to emerge in Bermuda. Perhaps in some prepared hideaway, already stocked with food, water, and weapons. But that didn't feel right. Stowing away was both passive and somehow unoriginal. It wasn't a personality fit. Ivan wouldn't risk the possibility of his legend ending with the headline, "Discovered by dogs."

Disguise was an option, but also risky. He'd have planned for the worst-case scenario, which had to include the yacht being surrounded and searched by competent pros. Hard men who would look twice and then again, regardless of whether the subject was wearing a ball gown, or surgical scrubs, or a police uniform.

That was the stumbling block.

A meticulous planner like Ivan would assume that everyone exiting the *Anzhelika* would be processed through a tight filter.

It was also the solution.

I knew where Ivan had gone.

I went down.

There was only one deck lower. The aft end of the bottom deck was occupied by fresh water storage and the engine room. Closer to the bow were the cold storage and wine cellar, where I'd begun the hunt. Descending the stairs I found myself further forward still. The trapezoidal room wasn't very deep, and it hummed with an odd gurgling mechanical noise. If my eyes had been closed I'd have been hard-pressed to place the sound, but they weren't, and the answer was right at my feet.

The C-Explorer submarine was a big glass sphere centered between the two arms of a C-shaped orange body. Looking like a pea wedged between a fork's two tines, the sphere was reminiscent of a helicopter cockpit, offering its occupants largely unobstructed views both horizontally and vertically. By the time I leapt down the last six stairs, only the top of the sphere still breached the water's surface.

"He's getting away by submarine," I yelled for the benefit of the mike.

If I'd had a gun, I could have shot the sphere, although I suspected most bullets would either pancake harmlessly or ricochet off what was no doubt the equivalent of bulletproof glass. But I didn't have a gun.

I scanned the room for weapons, but came up blank. Nothing but basic scuba gear.

Oscar said, "...ay ...ain ...les," which my brain translated to, "Say again, Achilles."

"He's about to launch a submarine off the bow!"

Oscar's reply translated to, "Say again. We're not reading you."

"Submarine!" Transmission was even worse than reception. They couldn't hear me. My signal wasn't penetrating all that steel. I had no time to fiddle with it. The sub was descending. What could they do anyway? As passionate as Director Rider was about killing The Ghost, he wasn't about to order a missile strike on Monaco.

I didn't have time to assemble the scuba equipment neatly stacked and stored in wall racks, so I checked the oxygen levels on the two used systems abandoned on the floor by pampered guests. The best read only one-third, good for about ten minutes. I grabbed its tank through the wet BCD's armholes, throwing it up and over and onto my back in the same single fluid motion I'd learned to use with backpacks. Then I slapped the

Velcro belt closed, grabbed a mask off the floor, and dove after the escaping sub.

Chapter 25

Flash Bang

IGNORING THE SEARING white flashes of pain and the concerned queries from the little girl's gawking mother, Jo pulled herself to her feet and continued her ascent.

No, she wasn't all right.

Yes, she needed a doctor.

But her needs would have to wait.

Each step set off an explosion in her foot, but each stair brought her closer. She didn't look down. She didn't want to see. It was enough to know that no matter what was there, she couldn't stop. Not until she had Michael. By the time she reached the top, her endorphins had kicked in and her Glock had come out.

Parting the blue curtain through which they'd watched Emily disappear an hour before, Jo spotted her prey. Michael was slipping into the driver's seat of his Mercedes, while the attentive valet held his door.

She almost cried with relief.

This was perfect!

She could hold Michael at gunpoint in his own car while calling Langley for instructions. They could even patch her through to Achilles. She hoped that he'd saved Emily and ended Ivan, but if not, capturing The Ghost's right-hand man would be some consolation. A reportable event. Food for Rider's PR machine.

Jo pushed all the pain from her body and pulled all her skills into play. She willed herself to be silent and invisible as she sprinted the short gap to the rear passenger door.

While the valet wished Michael a good evening, Jo slipped into his car. She was already positioned by the time Michael sat down. Arm raised, Glock aimed, game on.

Michael's door closed a second later with an incredibly loud bang, and a blinding white flash.

Chapter 26

Smug

AS I SPLASHED into the cool Mediterranean water, my hands made immediate contact with the back of the C-Explorer.

Then everything started to go wrong.

I couldn't find anything to grip, and my loose mask was filling with water, impeding the search. As the sub literally slipped through my fingers toward darkness and freedom, my lungs began screaming for air.

This couldn't be happening.

I wouldn't let it.

Ignoring the burning in my eyes and the panic in my lungs, I kicked and I stroked and I scanned and I prayed. Any second now, Ivan would engage the forward thrusters and vanish into the deep dark Mediterranean. I had to gain a handhold before he did.

After a few seconds of panicked searching and furious kicking, the *Anzhelika's* underwater lights revealed a prize. Like a shady palm tree on a desert oasis, a black handle protruded from the sphere's entry hatch.

If only I could reach it.

I was no kind of competitive swimmer, but cross-country skiing had given me an ox's heart, a dolphin's lungs, and a muscular system primed for sprinting. I set my eye on that finish line and gave it everything I had. I kicked harder and stroked faster, and I stretched and strained, while the tank wobbled and the mask fluttered and my lungs begged for air. Then a thousand tiny bubbles spewed from the sub's rear grid, and I knew the forward thruster had just been engaged.

It was now or never.

With a giant coordinated thrust that called on every major muscle in my body, I porpoised forward and made contact with the middle finger of my left hand. It wasn't much, just a single distal phalange. But for a climber it was plenty. I locked it down and levered my shoulders forward, catching a full grip with my right hand just as the C-Explorer began to bolt.

Air.

I needed air.

I swapped my right hand for my left on the grip, reaching back for my regulator.

It wasn't there. The usual sweeping retrieval move doesn't work when you're being dragged.

My screaming lungs were starting to spasm.

I fought back by clamping my mouth shut. Turning my head, I saw my regulator flapping around with the three other hoses like towed ropes. I tilted my shoulders until it was fluttering in the right place, then snatched it and pressed it to my mouth.

Oxygen never tasted so sweet.

I cycled through a few deep inhales, then snugged and cleared my mask before recceing my situation. We were humming through the water at what felt like a sprint, but was likely just the speed of jogging. The water was cool and getting colder. And dark. So very dark.

Yachts moored above on harbor buoys spotlit the sea with azure cones of light. Seen from below, it looked like the set of a science fiction movie. An alien invasion.

Now that I could breathe and see, I pulled myself forward and looked into the sphere. It glowed with the radiation of dozens of LED lights. Knobs and buttons and screens and panels gave it a living luminescence.

The Ghost turned his head and looked back.

I don't know what I expected to see on his face. Maybe fear, or anger, or nervous tension. But those weren't what I got. There in the bluish-white glow, The Ghost wore a grin of pure satisfaction.

It didn't compute.

He should be angry, furious even. His plan had been foiled for the first time ever, and now he had a live tail.

Comprehension struck me like a blow to the gut.

Ivan had actually mapped this out. He'd gamed this very scenario in his head. Probably weeks earlier. He'd done the proverbial math during extensive contingency planning. Now he was sitting smugly like a chess master who saw ten moves ahead, while I was just getting a feel for the board.

With a dismissive *shoo-bug* brush of his hand, Ivan turned back to the main control panel and began diving even deeper. As the lights disappeared ever further above and behind, I recalled from my scuba certification class that anything below 60 feet was considered deep, and 130 was the conventional limit. I had no idea how deep the Mediterranean got off the Monaco coast, but I was pretty sure it was a lot deeper than that.

The race was on, and I only had about a minute.

I had two options: drown Ivan, or get him to surface. To do either, I'd have to disable the sub, quickly and without tools.

I started looking around for things I could yank or kick or twist or release. Cords or plugs or cables or housings. The C-Explorer looked more streamlined than a Formula One racer. I supposed that when someone was manufacturing toys for billionaires, the smart marketers went big on sleek design. My hungry eyes found nothing of tactical value anywhere, including alternative grips.

I thought about trying to jam the propeller housings at an angle that would force the sub to the surface, but there were two of those and just one of me. Regardless, I couldn't see either from my topside position, and I had no means to descend.

That left the passenger hatch. It screwed shut using a wheel housed in a recession that was covered on the forward half, making it hydrodynamic. Translation: I wouldn't get a lot of leverage. But with no destructive tools, no choice of handhold, and no time, I had no alternative. I grabbed the wheel and started twisting.

It didn't resist.

I got it through half a revolution before Ivan reached up and back behind his head to grab the inside lever with his right hand.

Submarines were born as military vessels. Naval engineers had designed them to prevent exactly the maneuver I was attempting. They put spoked levers rather than wheels on the inside of hatches, specifically to provide superior leverage.

I put both hands on the wheel and then doubled over to brace my feet against the housing. I began to heave with my arms extended, using the muscles of my back and legs. The wheel gave an inch. Hand over hand I worked it like a tug-of-war, fighting for every inch as I worked it through most of a rotation.

Then two things happened at once.

Ivan stood up, and stopped the wheel by bracing it with his second hand.

And my air ran out.

I don't scare easily, but losing the ability to breathe really rattled my cage. One second I was breathing normally, no more conscious of the process than on land, and the next my lungs wouldn't inflate. There was nothing to pull. It was like someone slapped duct tape over my mouth and nose.

Instinctively, I looked up before looking back down. There was only blackness above. I could have been fifty-feet down, I could have been a hundred. Ivan's eyes said it all when I returned to the wheel, determined to overpower him. The leverage required to turn it from the outside just wasn't there. And the bastard knew it.

The sub had stopped moving when Ivan abandoned the controls to stand. With no need to hold on, I now had the freedom to use both of my hands. But I didn't reach for the wheel. I yanked the empty tank off my back and raised it over my head like a battering ram. I was going to attack the sphere.

I envisioned Emily's choking face, and thought about the anguish she surely felt. I pictured Oscar and Rider back at Langley, barking out orders from the comfort of plush leather chairs. I thought about Jo, and the possibility that she might now be dead. I bundled those emotions and fed them to the fire that now fueled the rage powering my arms, back, and shoulders. Then I brought the tank down between my legs with the full force of my furious anger. It smashed into the sphere with a metallic clank that rang like victory in my ears, and sent a flash of fear across Ivan's eyes.

But the glass didn't crack.

As my heart dropped, my lungs implored me to swim for the surface.

Hatred held me in place.

I unscrewed the regulator from the top of the tank, streamlining my improvised weapon and giving it a point. Raising it high over my head, I brought it down again and a third time, pounding the valve stem against the same spot on the sphere with the precision and force of an ironworker's hammer. I was expecting a crack and hoping for an implosion.

I got nothing.

For all my effort and emotion, I was only burning oxygen, and making noise.

Game over.

The last I saw of Ivan the Ghost, he was sporting a smug smile, and waving goodbye.

Chapter 27

Motivations

THE OFFICE of the Director of the Central Intelligence Agency is no oval, but it still stole a few pints of my breath. The first three things to catch my eye were an ornate oak desk that looked as weighty as the decisions made behind it, a framed American flag rescued from the ruins of the World Trade Center, and a long lineup of vanity photos with celebrities ranging from LeBron James to Donald Trump. The plush blue carpeting still smelled new, and I was standing on it.

"You let The Ghost escape," Rider said, his voice tinged with anger and wrought with scorn. "The bloody Russian's been a thorn in our side for eight years, and when we finally get a lead on him, you literally let him walk. You had him, and you let him go, contravening my direct order."

I found Director Rider's contemptuous expression similar to Ivan's last glance. Even with air in my lungs, however, this experience was worse. In part because he was right. In part because I couldn't fight back. Regardless of what I thought of Rider, I respected his position. So I stood there and took it, eyes forward and mouth shut.

"You may think you're on the side of the angels, because you saved a girl, but you're failing to see the big picture. What you did was weaken a nation, a nation that millions fought to make strong. You not only showed poor judgment, you demonstrated that you can't be counted on when the going gets tough. When the big decisions are called for, you, Agent Achilles, get squeamish. That's what Granger failed to foresee when he recruited you from a ski club rather than the Special Forces. I require more than skills. I require instincts, and attitude."

I said nothing.

This seemed to further perturb the director. "Do you have anything to say for yourself?"

I shifted my eyes to Rider's. He looked exactly like what he was: a seasoned politician comfortably seated behind a big desk. An armchair general pretending to lead from behind. "Sir, what is Agent Monfort's condition?"

"Agent Josephine Monfort? Yes, there's another mark on the debit side of your ledger. Were it not for a first-rate emergency medical team, you'd be responsible for adding her star to the lobby wall. As it stands, she'll make a full recovery. Physically, that is. Losing Ivan isn't going to help her career. Anything else you'd like to say?"

"No, sir."

"Very well. Agent Achilles, having disobeyed a direct order and proven yourself to be of no use to me, and thus to this agency, you're fired."

"No, sir."

"That wasn't a question."

"Something about this case bothered me from the very beginning."

Rider grabbed a letter-opener off his desk, a miniature broadsword, and began to slice the air with its handle pinched between forefinger and thumb. The sight reminded me of the last thing I'd pinched between those fingers — and a decision I'd never regret. "And what was that?" he asked. "What bothered you?"

"The big picture."

I paused for a second to let my words plant roots in the worry center of his mind. "For eight years, Ivan's been a ghost. So smooth and secretive that he's become a living legend. But then suddenly he supposedly made the mistake of using the same bank account twice. I don't buy it. Too basic and amateur for a man who's legendary for operating without a trace."

Rider spread his hands, palms up. "He was due for a mistake. One in eight years isn't bad. Of course his record makes the fact that you blew it all that much worse."

I kept my eyes locked on Rider's. "That doubt nagged at me until I met The Ghost face to face. Then it vanished. The reason there's not another criminal on the planet like Ivan is that he takes meticulous planning to the extreme. The Ghost has contingencies for his contingencies. He's the Gary Kasparov of crime, except that he only plays one or two matches a year. The idea that Ivan would make such a basic mistake is as preposterous as Kasparov losing at checkers."

Rider brought his hands back together with a clap. "And yet that's how we found him."

"I don't think so."

"You conducted the investigation yourself, former-agent Achilles." Rider's voice was calm and unwavering, but the corners of his eyes were pulling back a little.

"I conducted the investigation that followed from having the client's identity, not the investigation that led to it. His identity was provided to me. By you."

Rider leaned back, shaking his head. "I got it from the financial crimes division."

"And I'm sure you've arranged for someone there to back you up on that. Nonetheless, I asked myself how you really might have gotten a lead on The Ghost. That's where Ivan's nature entered the mix." I paused just to watch his expression.

"You became Director of the CIA only after two surprising events happened. First, the president's initial nominee suddenly withdrew his name, citing personal reasons. Then, the chairman of the Senate Intelligence Committee suddenly became your ardent supporter."

"That's the nature of politics. What's your point?"

"My point is the pattern. That pattern was about to repeat in the London mayoral election — not that anyone would notice. Who would ever think to compare them? Two different continents, two different positions."

"I've run out of patience with you, Achilles. What are you saying?"

"I'm saying you hired The Ghost. You hired him to secure your position, and at the same time, you hired him to sway the London mayoral election."

Rider continued shaking his head. "Why on Earth would I care who wins the London mayoral election?"

"I can't think of a single reason."

"Well then …" He began to stand.

"Which is exactly why you picked it. It's similar enough in scale to the CIA Directorship that The Ghost wouldn't blink at having them grouped together, but different enough that nobody would ever connect the two."

Rider plunked back into his chair. "You're not making sense. Why would I hire The Ghost to rig an election I care nothing about?"

It was my turn to enjoy myself, and I was going to savor every second. "That's the big question, isn't it? I have two good answers. The first was camouflage. Hire The Ghost to put you into office, and he'll know it was you, regardless of code names and numbered bank accounts. Hire him for a package deal, however, with two totally unrelated names, and Ivan wouldn't have a clue as to who had hired him, or why." I paused to soak up the moment. Then I pulled a letter from my back pocket.

"As clever as that tactic is, the second reason is my favorite because it was a two-for-one deal." I paused there, just to see if I could make veins appear on Rider's temples. It took three seconds. "I spent the past twenty-four hours doing a bit of investigation, while I still had my credentials. I didn't find any evidence of your looking into Ivan's banking, but I did find your extensive research on Aspinwall. The London contract wasn't about influencing British politics. The London contract was about setting Ivan up."

"That's preposterous."

"By killing Ivan shortly after coming to office, you would eliminate the only witness to your crime. You'd begin your tenure with a dramatic win, a win that would prove your past naysayers wrong and cause your future opponents to think twice. Strategically, it was brilliant. Admirable, even. You outwitted the president, the Senate, and one of the most notorious criminals of our time."

Rider swapped his mask of indignation for one of

pleasant indifference, a core item in the wardrobe of all career politicians. "If that were true, one might say it reflects the kind of operational mind this country needs at the helm of the CIA."

"One might. But not me."

"But not you." Rider chewed on that a moment. "Well, it's been interesting listening to the imagination of a disgraced and traumatized former agent, but as long as you're where you are and I'm where I am, this story will never amount to more than that. Unless you have evidence, of course?" His eyes went to the letter in my hand. He couldn't help it.

I shook my head and steeled myself for the smug smile to come — the last I ever intended to see. "You're where you are, and I'm where I am, and traumatized though I might be by the brutality of DC-league politics, I'm not naive enough to think that I could win that fight without a smoking gun. I'm also not corrupt enough to switch over to the dark side. Not yet, anyway."

"So?"

I left him hanging for a minute. Gave him the experience of operating without air. It was a victory of sorts, albeit transient and minor. Then I handed over the letter. "So, I've decided to get out while my self-respect is still intact. I've decided to resign."

That yanked the mask right off, exposing the complete package. Stretched lips, raised chin, and triumphant eyes.

I turned and walked for the door, an old life behind me, a new one ahead. As my hand hit the big brass knob, I spun about again. "Of course, since I figured out that you set Ivan up, you can be certain that he will too. Enjoy the rest of your life, Director."

Chapter 28

Epilogue

"EVEN AFTER my own experience, I still can't believe Michael shot you," Emily said. "He was such a gentleman."

Jo had just exchanged her hospital gown for her civilian clothes and was finally headed for the door when Emily surprised her. She'd walked right into her room, accompanied by a doctor whose lab coat read Lawrence Danton, M.D.

Jo had assumed that Emily was back in London, having heard that her physical wounds required little more than bandages and antiseptic. It was her psychological wounds that Jo had assumed would take time mending.

In answer to Emily's question, Jo unfastened the blouse buttons she'd done up just minutes before. Pulling the fabric aside like a wounded Superman, she exposed the center of her chest. Four weeks of top medical care had no doubt facilitated rapid healing, but the scar on her breastbone still appeared plenty angry. Perhaps it always would. "It looks bad, but I was incredibly lucky."

"You were unbelievably lucky," Doctor Danton said. "I just read through the notes on your chart."

Jo had been blessed no less than four times by her count. First, when the bullet expended most of its energy drilling through the Mercedes' seat. Second, when it hit her bony sternum rather than her soft flesh. Third, when the shock knocked her out so she appeared to be dead. And fourth, by avoiding head strikes and disfigurement when Michael dumped her from his moving car. The scrapes on her back and buttocks were severe enough to require skin grafts and a month-long convalescent stay. But thanks to her leather riding clothes, those were just flesh wounds, as the professional soldiers say.

"Doctor Danton took care of me when they brought me to the emergency room," Emily said, her voice unexpectedly enthusiastic. Whatever mood-altering medication they'd given her, Jo wanted some.

"We came to ask you about the man who saved me. Nobody seems to know who he is or what happened to him."

"Why are you asking me?" Jo asked, prevaricating. This was slippery territory.

"The police linked our cases through Michael. He brought me to the yacht show and took you away. Since the valet said you had a gun on him at the time, we know you were trying to stop him, just like that man was trying to stop Andreas, or Ivan, or whatever his name is. We know you told the police you don't know anything, and for some reason they appear to have lost all interest, but we were hoping you'd tell me. Girl to girl. Given that shared scars are a special kind of bond."

Jo knew the police had lost interest because they'd been ordered to. But she'd have expected Emily's father to use his clout to get answers. Perhaps he had things he considered more important on his plate. "Why do you want to know about him?"

"To thank him, of course. I owe him my life."

Jo was a bit slow on account of the pain medication she'd been taking. But she put it together now. Emily had been speaking in first-person plural. *We* came to ask you. *We* know. *We* were hoping. And her tone. Her lively, joyful tone. "Are the two of you dating?"

Emily reached down and took Doctor Danton's hand. "The day that necklace punctured my trachea was the luckiest of my life," she said.

Well, stone the crows, Jo thought. Given all the time she had to kill while confined to a recovery bed, Jo had spent hours worrying about Emily's post-traumatic psychological condition. She hadn't reached out herself for fear of what she'd find, fear that Achilles' sacrifice would have been wasted saving someone who no longer wanted to live.

Still stalling for time to think, she asked, "Does this mean you're not going back to London anytime soon? The papers report that it's soon to be an Aspinwall town."

"Home is where the heart is. Will you tell me about him, please?"

Jo wasn't sure what to say. She knew Achilles had resigned, but little more. The rumor mill was far less active in The Agency than in almost every other institution, but people were still people, and gossip was a force all its own, as irrepressible as the American people themselves. Some said Achilles refused to work for Director Rider, others that he'd been fired. "So you're happy?" she asked Emily.

"The happiest I've ever been."

Jo wasn't sure that would last, but it was clear that Emily meant it. "Well, that's all the thanks he'd ever want."

"But who is he? Where is he?"

"I honestly don't know where he is. As for who, well, he's the guy who comes calling, when good people like you are in need."

AUTHOR'S NOTE

Dear Reader,

THANK YOU for reading *Chasing Ivan*. I hope you enjoyed it. If you would be so kind as to take a moment to leave a review on Amazon or elsewhere, I would be very grateful. Reviews and referrals are as vital to an author's success as a good GPA is to a student's.

I know this can be a bit of a pain, so if you do write a review or share the experience via your social network, please email me at tim@timtigner.com so I can "like" your post and e-mail you a link to some amazing Achilles-style climbing videos as a token of my gratitude.

With best regards,

Also in the Kyle Achilles series

Pushing Brilliance, The Lies of Spies,
Falling Stars, Twist and Turn

The Achilles story continues with

PUSHING BRILLIANCE

Turn the page for a preview . . .

PUSHING BRILLIANCE

Chapter 1

The Kremlin

HOW DO YOU PITCH an audacious plan to the most powerful man in the world? Grigori Barsukov was about to find out.

Technically, the President of Russia was an old friend — although the last time they'd met, his old friend had punched him in the face. That was thirty years ago, but the memory remained fresh, and Grigori's nose still skewed to the right.

Back then, he and President Vladimir Korovin wore KGB lieutenant stars. Now both were clothed in the finest Italian suits. But his former roommate also sported the confidence of one who wielded unrivaled power, and the temper of a man ruthless enough to obtain it.

The world had spun on a different axis when they'd

worked together, an east-west axis, running from Moscow to Washington. Now everything revolved around the West. America was the sole superpower.

Grigori could change that.

He could lever Russia back into a pole position.

But only if his old rival would risk joining him — way out on a limb.

As Grigori's footfalls fell into cadence with the boots of his escorts, he coughed twice, attempting to relax the lump in his throat. It didn't work. When the hardwood turned to red carpet, he willed his palms to stop sweating. They didn't listen. Then the big double doors rose before him and it was too late to do anything but take a deep breath, and hope for the best.

The presidential guards each took a single step to the side, then opened their doors with crisp efficiency and a click of their heels. Across the office, a gilded double-headed eagle peered down from atop the dark wood paneling, but the lone living occupant of the Kremlin's inner sanctum did not look up.

President Vladimir Korovin was studying photographs.

Grigori stopped three steps in as the doors were closed behind him, unsure of the proper next move. He wondered if everyone felt this way the first time. Should he stand at attention until acknowledged? Take a seat by the wall?

He strolled to the nearest window, leaned his left

shoulder up against the frame, and looked out at the Moscow River. Thirty seconds ticked by with nothing but the sound of shifting photos behind him. Was it possible that Korovin still held a grudge?

Desperate to break the ice without looking like a complete fool, he said, "This is much nicer than the view from our academy dorm room."

Korovin said nothing.

Grigori felt his forehead tickle. Drops of sweat were forming, getting ready to roll. As the first broke free, he heard the stack of photos being squared, and then at long last, the familiar voice. It posed a very unfamiliar question: "Ever see a crocodile catch a rabbit?"

Grigori whirled about to meet the Russian President's gaze. "What?"

Korovin waved the stack of photos. His eyes were the same cornflower blue Grigori remembered, but their youthful verve had yielded to something darker. "I recently returned from Venezuela. Nicolas took me crocodile hunting. Of course, we didn't have all day to spend on sport, so our guides cheated. They put rabbits on the riverbank, on the wide strip of dried mud between the water and the tall grass. Kind of like teeing up golf balls. Spaced them out so the critters couldn't see each other and gave each its own pile of alfalfa while we watched in silence from an electric boat." Korovin was clearly enjoying the telling of his intriguing tale. He gestured with broad sweeps as he spoke, but kept his eyes locked on Grigori.

"Nicolas told me these rabbits were brought in special from the hill country, where they'd survived a thousand generations amidst foxes and coyotes. When you put them on the riverbank, however, they're completely clueless. It's not their turf, so they stay where they're dropped, noses quivering, ears scanning, eating alfalfa and watching the wall of vegetation in front of them while crocodiles swim up silently from behind.

"The crocodiles were being fooled like the rabbits, of course. Eyes front, focused on food. Oblivious." Korovin shook his head as though bewildered. "Evolution somehow turned a cold-blooded reptile into a warm white furball, but kept both of the creature's brains the same. Hard to fathom. Anyway, the capture was quite a sight.

"Thing about a crocodile is, it's a log one moment and a set of snapping jaws the next, with nothing but a furious blur in between. One second the rabbit is chewing alfalfa, the next second the rabbit is alfalfa. Not because it's too slow or too stupid ... but because it's out of its element."

Grigori resisted the urge to swallow.

"When it comes to eating," Korovin continued, "crocs are like storybook monsters. They swallow their food whole. Unlike their legless cousins, however, they want it dead first. So once they've trapped dinner in their maw, they drag it underwater to drown it. This means the rabbit is usually alive and uninjured in the croc's mouth for a while — unsure what the hell just happened, but pretty damn certain it's not good."

The president leaned back in his chair, placing his feet on the desk and his hands behind his head. He was having fun.

Grigori felt like the rabbit.

"That's when Nicolas had us shoot the crocs. After they clamped down around the rabbits, but before they dragged 'em under. That became the goal, to get the rabbit back alive."

Grigori nodded appreciatively. "Gives a new meaning to the phrase, catch and release."

Korovin continued as if Grigori hadn't spoken. "The trick was putting a bullet directly into the croc's tiny brain, preferably the medulla oblongata, right there where the spine meets the skull. Otherwise the croc would thrash around or go under before you could get off the kill shot, and the rabbit was toast.

"It was good sport, and an experience worth replicating. But we don't have crocodiles anywhere near Moscow, so I've been trying to come up with an equally engaging distraction for my honored guests. Any ideas?"

Grigori felt like he'd been brought in from the hills. The story hadn't helped the lump in his throat either. He managed to say, "Let me give it some thought."

Korovin just looked at him expectantly.

Comprehension struck after an uncomfortable silence. "What happened to the rabbits?"

Korovin returned his feet to the floor, and leaned forward in his chair. "Good question. I was curious to see that myself. I put my first survivor back on the riverbank beside a fresh pile of alfalfa. It ran for the tall grass as if I'd lit its tail on fire. That rabbit had learned life's most important lesson."

Grigori bit. "What's that?"

"Doesn't matter where you are. Doesn't matter if you're a crocodile or a rabbit. You best look around, because you're never safe.

"Now, what have you brought me, Grigori?"

Grigori breathed deeply, forcing the reptiles from his mind. He pictured his future atop a corporate tower, an oligarch on a golden throne. Then he spoke with all the gravitas of a wedding vow. "I brought you a plan, Mister President."

Chapter 2

Brillyanc

PRESIDENT KOROVIN REPEATED Grigori's assertion aloud. "You brought me a plan." He paused for a long second, as though tasting the words.

Grigori felt like he was looking up from the Colosseum floor after a gladiator fight. Would the emperor's thumb point up, or down?

Korovin was savoring the power. Finally, the president gestured toward the chess table abutting his desk, and Grigori's heart resumed beating.

The magnificent antique before which Grigori took a seat was handcrafted of the same highly polished hardwood as Korovin's desk, probably by a French craftsman now centuries dead. Korovin took the opposing chair and pulled a chess clock from his drawer. Setting it on the table, he pressed the button that activated Grigori's timer. "Give me the three-minute version."

Grigori wasn't a competitive chess player, but like any Russian who had risen through government ranks, he was familiar with the sport.

Chess clocks have two timers controlled by

seesawing buttons. When one's up, the other's down, and vice versa. After each move, a player slaps his button, stopping his timer and setting his opponent's in motion. If a timer runs out, a little red plastic flag drops, and that player loses. Game over. There's the door. Thank you for playing.

Grigori planted his elbows on the table, leaned forward, and made his opening move. "While my business is oil and gas, my hobby is investing in startups. The heads of Russia's major research centers all know I'm a so-called angel investor, so they send me their best early-stage projects. I get everything from social media software, to solar power projects, to electric cars.

"A few years ago, I met a couple of brilliant biomedical researchers out of Kazan State Medical University. They had applied modern analytical tools to the data collected during tens of thousands of medical experiments performed on political prisoners during Stalin's reign. They were looking for factors that accelerated the human metabolism — and they found them. Long story short, a hundred million rubles later I've got a drug compound whose strategic potential I think you'll appreciate."

Grigori slapped his button, pausing his timer and setting the president's clock in motion. It was a risky move. If Korovin wasn't intrigued, Grigori wouldn't get to finish his pitch. But Grigori was confident that his old roommate was hooked. Now he would have to admit as much if he wanted to hear the rest.

The right side of the president's mouth contracted back a couple millimeters. A crocodile smile. He slapped the clock. "Go on."

"The human metabolism converts food and drink into the fuel and building blocks our bodies require. It's an exceptionally complex process that varies greatly from individual to individual, and within individuals over time. Metabolic differences mean some people naturally burn more fat, build more muscle, enjoy more energy, and think more clearly than others. This is obvious from the locker room to the boardroom to the battlefield. The doctors in Kazan focused on the mental aspects of metabolism, on factors that improved clarity of thought–"

Korovin interrupted, "Are you implying that my metabolism impacts my IQ?"

"Sounds a little funny at first, I know, but think about your own experience. Don't you think better after coffee than after vodka? After salad than fries? After a jog and a hot shower than an afternoon at a desk? All those actions impact the mental horsepower you enjoy at any given moment. What my doctors did was figure out what the body needs to optimize cognitive function."

"Something other than healthy food and sufficient rest?"

Perceptive question, Grigori thought. "Picture your metabolism like a funnel, with raw materials such as food and rest going in the top, cognitive power coming out the bottom, and dozens of complex metabolic processes in between."

"Okay," Korovin said, eager to engage in a battle of wits.

"Rather than following in the footsteps of others by attempting to modify one of the many metabolic processes, the doctors in Kazan took an entirely different approach, a brilliant approach. They figured out how to widen the narrow end of the funnel."

"So, bottom line, the brain gets more fuel?"

"Generally speaking, yes."

"With what result? Will every day be like my best day?"

"No," Grigori said, relishing the moment. "Every day will be better than your best day."

Korovin cocked his head. "How much better?"

Who's the rabbit now? "Twenty IQ points."

"Twenty points?"

"Tests show that's the average gain, and that it applies across the scale, regardless of base IQ. But it's most interesting at the high end."

Another few millimeters of smile. "Why is the high end the most interesting?"

"Take a person with an IQ of 140. Give him Brillyanc — that's the drug's name — and he'll score

160. May not sound like a big deal, but roughly speaking, those 20 points take his IQ from 1 in 200, to 1 in 20,000. Suddenly, instead of being the smartest guy in the room, he's the smartest guy in his discipline."

Korovin leaned forward and locked on Grigori's eyes. "Every ambitious scientist, executive, lawyer ... and politician would give his left nut for that competitive advantage. Hell, his left and right."

Grigori nodded.

"And it really works?"

"It really works."

Korovin reached out and leveled the buttons, stopping both timers and pausing to think, his left hand still resting on the clock. "So your plan is to give Russians an intelligence edge over foreign competition? Kind of analogous to what you and I used to do, all those years ago."

Grigori shook his head. "No, that's not my plan."

The edges of the cornflower eyes contracted ever so slightly. "Why not?"

"Let's just say, widening the funnel does more than raise IQ."

Korovin frowned and leaned back, taking a moment to digest this twist. "Why have you brought this to me, Grigori?"

"As I said, Mister President, I have a plan I think you're going to like."

ABOUT THE AUTHOR

Tim Tigner began his career in Soviet Counterintelligence with the US Army Special Forces, the Green Berets. That was back in the Cold War days when, "We learned Russian so you didn't have to," something he did at the Presidio of Monterey alongside Recon Marines and Navy SEALs.

With the fall of the Berlin Wall, Tim switched from espionage to arbitrage. Armed with a Wharton MBA rather than a Colt M16, he moved to Moscow in the midst of Perestroika. There, he led prominent multinational medical companies, worked with cosmonauts on the MIR Space Station (from Earth, alas), chaired the Association of International Pharmaceutical Manufacturers, and helped write Russia's first law on healthcare.

Moving to Brussels during the formation of the EU, Tim ran Europe, Middle East, and Africa for a Johnson & Johnson company and traveled like a character in a Robert Ludlum novel. He eventually landed in Silicon Valley, where he launched new medical technologies as a startup CEO.

In his free time, Tim has climbed the peaks of Mount Olympus, went hang gliding from the cliffs of Rio de Janeiro, and ballooned over Belgium. He earned scuba certification in Turkey, learned to ski in Slovenia, and ran the Serengeti with a Maasai warrior. He acted on-stage in Portugal, taught negotiations in Germany, and chaired a healthcare conference in Holland. Tim studied psychology in France, radiology in England, and philosophy in Greece. He has enjoyed ballet at the Bolshoi, the opera on Lake Como, and the symphony in Vienna. He's been a marathoner, paratrooper, triathlete, and yogi.

Intent on combining his creativity with his experience, Tim began writing thrillers in 1996 from an apartment overlooking Moscow's Gorky Park. Twenty years later, his passion for creative writing continues to grow every day. His home office now overlooks a vineyard in Northern California, where he lives with his wife Elena and their two daughters.

Tim grew up in the Midwest, and graduated from Hanover College with a BA in Philosophy and Mathematics. After military service and work as a financial analyst and foreign-exchange trader, he earned an MBA in Finance and an MA in International Studies from the Wharton and Lauder Schools of the University of Pennsylvania.

Thank you for taking the time to read about the author. Tim is most grateful for his loyal fans, and loves to correspond with readers like you. You are welcome to reach him directly at tim@timtigner.com.

ACKNOWLEDGEMENTS

Writing novels full of twists and turns is relatively easy. Doing so logically and coherently while maintaining a rapid pace is much tougher. Surprising readers without confusing them is the real art.

And then there are the characters….

I'm grateful to the Editors and Beta Readers of *Chasing Ivan* for their guidance with the finer points of plot and character, and for their assistance in fighting my natural inclination toward typos.

R. James Bishop, Doug Branscombe, Ian Cockerill, Denny Eckstein, Geof Ferrell, Emily Hagman, Robert Lawrence, Margaret Lovett, Tony McCafferty, Joe McKinley, Bill Overton, Stan Resnicoff, Chris Seelbach, Todd Simpson, Marsha Stutsman, and Slaven Tomasi.

Made in the USA
San Bernardino, CA
27 April 2019